THE OUTLAWED

Ray Hogan is an author who has inspired a loyal following over the years since he published his first Western novel *Ex-marshal* in 1956. Hogan was born in Willow Springs, Missouri, where his father was town marshal. At five the Hogan family moved to Albuquerque where Ray Hogan still lives in the foothills of the Sandia and Manzano mountains. His father was on the Albuquerque police force and, in later years, owned the Overland Hotel. It was while listening to his father and other old-timers tell tales from the past that Ray was inspired to recast these tales in fiction. From the beginning he did exhaustive research into the history and the people of the Old West and the walls of his study are lined with various firearms, spurs, pictures, books, and memorabilia, about all of which he can talk in dramatic detail. Among his most popular works are the series of books about Shawn Starbuck, a searcher in a quest for a lost brother, who has a clear sense of right and wrong and who is willing to stand up and be counted when it is a question of fairness or justice. His other major series is about lawman John Rye whose reputation has earned him the sobriquet 'The Doomsday Marshal'. 'I've attempted to capture the courage and bravery of those men and women that lived out West and the dangers and problems they had to overcome,' Hogan once remarked. If his lawmen protagonists seem sometimes larger than life, it is because they are men of integrity, heroes who through grit of character and common sense are able to overcome the obstacles they encounter despite often overwhelming odds. This same grit of character can also be found in Hogan's heroines and, in *The Vengeance of Fortuna West*, Hogan wrote a gripping and totally believable account of a woman who takes up the badge and tracks the men who killed her lawman husband by ambush. No less intriguing in her way is Nellie Dupray, convicted of rustling in *The Glory Trail*. Above all, what is most impressive about Hogan's Western novels is the consistent quality with which each is crafted, the compelling depth of his characters, and his ability to juxtapose the complexities of human conflict into narratives always as intensely interesting as they are emotionally involving. His latest novel is *Soldier in Buckskin*.

THE OUTLAWED

Ray Hogan

GUNSMOKE

First published in the US by Signet Books

This hardback edition 2011
by AudioGO Ltd
by arrangement with
Golden West Literary Agency

ISBN 978 1 445 85684 1

British Library Cataloguing in Publication Data available.

Printed and bound in Great Britain by
MPG Books Group Limited

1

As the lean, coppery figure of the Apache rose suddenly from the tall brush fringing the trail—dark face contorted, black eyes glittering with hate—Shawn Starbuck reacted instinctively. Lunging to one side, he avoided the slash of the brave's knife, and reaching for the pistol on his hip, threw himself backwards off the saddle.

He struck the sandy earth hard, thorny brush raking him savagely, carving red runnels across his arms, his face. Smothering a curse, he rolled away, barely escaping the blade again as the Apache sprang upon him, bore him down. Heaving with all his strength, he partly dislodged the sweaty body, lashed out with the forty-five clamped in his hand.

The barrel connected with the brave's skull, made a dull thudding sound. The knife fell to the sand, and for a moment the muscular, crouching figure above him seemed to waver; and then Starbuck felt strong fingers close about his throat. Frantically he grabbed the Apache's wrist, pulled, seeking to break the tightening grip, while through the swirling dust he could see the brave's free arm upraised, a stone hatchet poised to strike.

Desperate, Starbuck jerked his head to one side, kneed the straddling Indian hard in the back. As the tomahawk swished by his ear, buried itself in the soil, he humped his body quickly, rocked the brave off balance, and holding tight to the pistol jammed the barrel deep into the Indian's groin, all the while sucking deep for breath.

The buck groaned in a wild sort of way, fell back. Starbuck, no longer encumbered by the fingers at his throat, struck again with the heavy weapon. The blow caught the Apache across the bridge of his plowshare nose, cracked ominously.

The brave gasped, sagged weakly. Instantly Starbuck

swung again, now holding the pistol by its barrel, using the butt as a deadly club . . . it would be simple to pull the trigger, blast all life from the Apache in a single fragment of time and thus end it, but such might be a mistake. Likely the brave was not alone, and a gunshot echoing across the hills and arroyos could serve to bring other copper warriors down upon him.

The blow went true, caving in the Apache's skull. He wilted soundlessly, the muscles of his lithe body relaxing, his eyes glazing as he slid quietly onto the hot sand.

Shawn lay completely motionless, muffling the sound of his labored breathing, listening into the searing heat of the August afternoon. Sweat and dust caked his body, blurred his vision. He had an overpowering urge to rise, scrub at his eyes, clear his mouth, spit, but he turned away the impulse, waited. If there were other braves nearby who had heard the struggle, they would be coming, working their way in silently, cautiously.

The minutes dragged by under the scorching sun. A quarter hour . . . a half . . . his ears had caught no sound. Slowly, carefully, he raised his head a couple of inches off the hot sand, looking first for his horse—his sole hope of getting out of the area fast if compelled to make a run for it. He breathed a little easier.

The sorrel, a horse he had recently traded his ailing chestnut gelding for, badly frightened and shying off when the Apache had risen like some fearful specter from the brush, had raced off ten yards or so and then halted in a slight depression on the plateau, was now picking disinterestedly at the scanty growth along its edges. He would not be hard to reach.

And Shawn reckoned he'd damn well better do just that —assuming the opportunity presented itself. A couple of more tussles with renegade Apaches, such as this, and there'd be a good chance he'd never make it to Lynchburg, where he planned to look up a man named Jim Ivory who, hopefully, was his long-missing brother.

He'd gotten wind of this Jim Ivory up New Mexico way from a cowhand who thought Ivory fit the description of Ben Starbuck, such as it was, that Shawn had given him. It was slim, of course; it had been a full ten years since Shawn last saw his older brother, and there wasn't much he could go on.

Actually, he had ridden all the way from Kansas to see the cowhand he'd spoken with—a man who's name was Henry Smith—in the belief that he was Ben. But as had

6

been the case in a dozen or more previous instances when he had gone chasing across the frontier on the strength of a tip, the lead had proved a false one. Henry Smith, while resembling the mind's-eye picture Shawn had of his brother, had not been him.

In the ensuing conversation, however, Smith had mentioned a man he'd worked with on a ranch in Arizona's Mogollon country—a fellow called Jim Ivory. He fit the description, Henry Smith had declared, and it might be worth Shawn's time to ride down, look the man over, and have a talk with him—if he didn't mind the hard trip.

Starbuck didn't. He never passed up the smallest lead, for until he found Ben, who had run away from home at sixteen to escape their iron-fisted father, Hiram, the Starbuck estate was in suspense and the thirty thousand dollars lying in the vault of an Ohio bank could be touched by no one. Half the money was Shawn's, but the will directed he must find his brother before claiming his share.

In the beginning it had been a sort of lark to the young farm boy, a wandering about that started first at a point on the Mexico-Texas border where he had recalled Ben once professed a wish to go. Arriving there and finding his brother had long since moved on, he then began an arduous but resolute quest directed only by rumors, the vague and unreliable memories of men he chanced to encounter—and pure hunches.

Eventually the novelty wore off and to the farm boy, still young but developed now into a tall, gray-eyed range rider of serious mien, the search became a way of life, one that ofttimes appeared to be leading nowhere and accomplishing nothing other than to store within him a wealth of experience and knowledge of the vast land he crisscrossed and the people he encountered.

And it brought to him many times, as he sat on a hilltop and gazed down upon a quiet ranch house where lamplight laid soft, yellow squares against the darkness, or watched smoke curling upward from some homesteader's simple cabin, that his was a rootless sort of existence; that he also had accumulated nothing—not even friends, since those persons, met once, were only acquaintances not likely ever to cross his path again.

One day he knew it would all come to an end, and if asked what he had to show for the lifetime a tolerant Creator had granted him on earth, he could give no answer, for he felt there was none.

Oh, there were those he'd had occasion to lend a hand and give aid to in their time of stress and trouble, but

7

Shawn Starbuck considered such unworthy of special note, since, to him, to assist another at such moment was in the nature of duty—his duty as a human being. He could see no logic in accepting acclaim when he had done only what was right—what he believed any other man would have done had he been presented with a similar set of circumstances. And to those involved who looked at it differently and sought to thank him, he had, almost shyly, turned a deaf ear and ridden on, pricked by some strange sort of embarrassment.

Just as each man is stirred by a different tune, and lives by his own set of values, Shawn, the product of an idealistic schoolteacher mother and a hard-bitten, practical, son-of-the-soil father, was no exception to that principle; he lived by a code that had been painstakingly instilled within him by that unlikely duo and saw no reason to take glory for something he considered the simple obligation of one man to another.

He glanced at the Apache. Indians were on the move again—he'd heard that as far back as Magdalena, had seen evidence of the fact as he'd ridden deeper into Arizona on a southwesterly course that led him between the landmarks of St. Peter's Dome and Green's Peak and on to Big Mountain; from there he altered course slightly, now faced directly into the sunset, came finally to the Corduroy River and the Big Butte country where he presently was.

The great, forbidding Mogollon Mountains, like a vast, dark barrier flung up against the clean sky, were to his right here—the north, and from that he knew he was drawing near journey's end. Soon he'd enter the Rockinstraw Valley, then would come Lynchburg, and twenty miles or so outside that settlement he would find the Box C Ranch where Jim Ivory worked.

He had stalled long enough. No other Apaches had appeared. It could be the buck was alone, but he still had his doubts as to that. Ordinarily they ran in parties, preferring to hunt both man and game in the company of fellow braves. Again Shawn lifted his head, swept the surrounding country with a hard, thrusting glance.

Nothing. From where he lay, however, he could not see into the broad basin on ahead. There could be others there. If so, he could take comfort from the thought that they were unaware of his presence on the little plateau, otherwise they would have closed in on him by now.

He'd be a fool to wait around any longer. The dead brave would be missed and a search instituted. Drawing

8

his legs up beneath him, Shawn brushed sweat from his eyes and slowly came to a crouched position. Instantly he froze as motion down in the basin, now within his line of vision, caught his attention.

An Apache brave, sun gleaming on his near-naked body, was directly in front of him in the brush-and-rock-littered sink less than a hundred paces away. The buck halted, became an immobile bronze statue as he listened intently for something—or someone.

There were more. Shawn's eyes, narrowed to cut down the blinding glare, picked up movement a short distance below the first brave. He saw three more along the opposite edge of the basin. Only two carried rifles; the others had feathered lances, or, like the one who had attacked him, a stone tomahawk and a knife.

They seemed to be working toward a central point, as if closing in on some objective. The brave he had stumbled on had evidently been part of a shrinking circle.

Starbuck frowned, again swiped at the sweat clothing his face, blurring his vision. What were they after? He could see nothing, no one in that tortured welter of blistered rock and starved, shoulder-high brush. But there was a reason—there had to be.

Speculation came to a full stop. A man, dust-gray in the driving heat, head down and slightly staggering, broke into view. He was leading a starved-looking bay horse that favored its left foreleg.

The question cleared instantly for Shawn; the Apaches were after the rider with the lame horse, were allowing him to work out onto a small flat a short distance ahead where he would not have protection of the rocks and dense brush.

One of the braves with a rifle could have handled the problem at any point without difficulty, but they were wasting no bullets. Such were precious, hard to come by. It was much more practical to hold back, permit the lone white man to reach the open where a lance would be as accurate and every bit as deadly.

Starbuck hunched lower, crossed swiftly to a thick clump of cedar. From that screened position he had a much more complete view of the basin. Crouched, he took it all in—the slowly unfolding drama of violence as the solitary, unsuspecting man, in a bad way himself, leading his crippled horse over the rough, broken ground, moved deeper into the gradually tightening noose of Apache braves.

Shawn brushed at his jaw, glanced to where the sorrel

9

was grazing. It would be a simple matter to drop back, work his way down the slight incline to the gelding, and mount up. By keeping well away from the rim of the sink he could continue his way unseen, soon put himself well in the clear of all danger in the basin.

He brushed the thought aside. He had to consider the gaunt stranger and his horse. The man had ten, possibly fifteen more minutes of life remaining unless he was warned—and given help. The problem was how to reach him in time, stop him while he was still in the comparative shelter of the brush.

Starbuck turned away, dropped back quickly to the sorrel. Thrusting a toe into the stirrup, he sprang to the saddle. For a moment he sat there, studying the land from his elevated vantage point, and then, again brushing at the salty brine clouding his eyes, wheeled the red gelding about and doubled back up the draw, across the flinty little plateau where the dead Apache lay, and angled for the upper end of the sink.

By coming in from above he should be able to reach the doomed man without the Indians being aware of his presence. At least, he hoped that was the way it would work out.

2

A narrow trail led off to the right of the plateau, going down into the sink. He bypassed it, realizing it would take him down onto a level with the Apaches, and place him opposite rather than behind the man he sought to help, and so continued on.

Abruptly the flat dropped off into another fairly deep gully. He rode into it, cut right, and shortly entered the brush fringing the sink. The rider was below him now, but he could not be certain the same was true of all the Apaches; he had no idea how many braves were skulking about in the basin—how large the living noose that was tightening around its intended victim. He could only guess.

He gave thought to dismounting to improve his chances for passing unseen through the undergrowth, then dropped the idea. He would be moving slower if such a plan were followed, and time was running out for the stranger. He had to be stopped before he got beyond the protection of the rocks and brush.

Bent forward on the saddle, Shawn urged the gelding on, keeping to the narrow aisles between the rank growth and mounds of boulders. He saw no indication of additional braves, but took no confidence from that; he saw no horses either, knowing well the Apache's ponies were somewhere nearby. If they could be successfully hidden, so could several more warriors.

The sorrel's ears flicked suddenly as he paused in stride. Starbuck drew in instantly, the understanding between man and horse strong. The gelding had seen something he, himself, had missed. For a few moments he remained motionless in the heat-blasted depths of the brush-filled sink, listening, probing the undergrowth with careful eyes.

He could neither hear nor see anything suspicious. It could have been a bird veering through the shadows, or possibly a rabbit scampering out from beneath the sorrel's hooves.

11

Lifting the leathers a bit, he started the gelding forward, now at a slower gait and with more thought to silence. He couldn't be far behind the man with the lame horse, and if the Apaches had worked in, closed the loop, there was every possibility there'd be two or three of them ahead.

Starbuck saw the brave a split second before the coppery warrior, hearing the muted sound of the sorrel's tread on the loose sand, wheeled. The Indian's eyes flared in surprise and alarm; his mouth opened to yell just as Shawn, leaving the saddle in a low dive, hit him full on.

The brave went down in a flailing of arms and legs. A stifled cry escaped his lips despite Starbuck's fingers clamped about his throat, and then there was a muffled groan as Shawn, again using the forty-five, clubbed him hard on the side of the head.

Instantly Starbuck was on his feet. He'd silenced the buck—but not soon enough. That one strangled sound would have been heard by others. They would hesitate, wonder, and then one or two were certain to investigate. He had only moments left now to reach the man somewhere just ahead, voice a warning, and then quickly find a suitable place where, together, they could make a stand.

He swore silently, dashing at the sweat. If he could just yell—call out! But that was out of the question; there were the Apaches in the remainder of the circle to remember —and hopefully keep at a distance until safety was reached.

The lame horse was suddenly before him. In the same instant he saw the dusty, dejected figure of the man. They were still in the brush, only paces from the clearing where the Apaches would undoubtedly strike.

Starbuck halted, emitted a low whistle, pivoted to glance about, seeking a place where they could pull off and find some degree of protection. A butte to his right offered possibilities. It would give them something to their backs, and a fairly good-sized boulder would serve as a rampart in front.

He swung his attention again to the rider. The man had halted, studied him with dull suspicion. His worn, pinched face was florid, marked with even brighter red splotches where the pitiless sun had left its mark on skin unaccustomed to stringency; it was a face that appeared too old for a body that could be no more than ten years Shawn's senior.

"Apaches—all around us!" Starbuck called in a hoarse whisper. "This way—we'll make a stand at that bluff," he added, pointing.

Immediately he turned the sorrel for the reddish formation, urging him with a steady pressure of his rowels. Halfway he glanced at the rider. The man had not stirred. Impatience flared through Shawn.

"Come on—dammit! They're closing in on you!"

In the next breath a lance, its feathers swirling brightly in the hot sunlight, soared across the open ground, struck point down and quivering an arm's length back of the lame horse. The man delayed no longer. Pivoting, he started for the bluff at an awkward run.

Starbuck, reaching the formation, hit the ground fast as the basin came alive with the yells of Indians. He saw a brave dart from a clump of brush a few steps beyond the rider, race toward him. Sunlight glinted on the shining steel blade of the knife clutched in his hand. Taking cool, deliberate aim with his forty-five, Shawn dropped the brave in his tracks.

In the next moment man and horse were behind the rock, the rider dropping the reins as the bay sidled anxiously up to the sorrel as if seeking kindred companionship, while the haggard traveler, pistol in hand, took a place next to Starbuck at the boulder.

Shawn, eyes sweeping restlessly back and forth, taking in both sides of the area fronting the bluff, swore deeply. Suddenly there were no Apaches—not even any yells. The braves had disappeared completely; it was as if it had all been an illusion. But they were there, silent as dark shadows, reorganizing, getting themselves set and planning their next move. There were two white men now.

"Obliged to you, mister," the rider murmured in a dry, raspy voice. He swallowed noisily as if speaking was a chore.

Shawn shrugged. "Spotted you from above. Had you surrounded and I figured I'd better set in on the game. . . . My name's Starbuck—Shawn Starbuck."

"Mine's—uh, Mason. You get jumped doing it?"

Shawn's glance followed Mason's line of vision. There was a streak of blood on his forearm, more on his sleeve.

"Bumped into a couple. Keep watching the left. I'll take the right—and we'd both best keep an eye out straight ahead. They'll be hitting us again—soon as they figure out our weak spot."

"Whole damned place is a weak spot," Mason said, looking around.

"Won't argue that—and I sure didn't pick it on purpose! One thing for certain, we've got to get out of here before dark."

13

Mason was silent for a time, then: "How many Apaches did you spot?"

"Eight, maybe ten. Hard to tell, way they were moving in and out of the brush."

"A God's plenty of them. No way I can see that we can get away from that big a party."

The defeat in Mason's attitude and voice was evident. A man who's been through hell a couple of times, Shawn thought, and wondered if it had come about from being in the war; but the war had been over for ten years; you'd think a man could have shaken the terrible memories that possessed him in that length of time.

He slid another glance at Mason, now turned from him, eyes on the brush and patches of open ground below. He had thin, straw-colored hair badly in need of trimming. His clothing—pants and shirt—were of some sleazy material, coarse and ill-fitting. His boots were worn, although the heels appeared to have been repaired recently. The pistol in his gnarled hand was an old Colt forty-four-caliber Walker. No rifle was slung from his saddle.

"Answer's to get ourselves up and out of this sink," Starbuck said, replying to the man's resigned comment. "We make it to the flat above us, chances for slipping off are plenty good."

Mason twisted about, looked to the rim above them. "How'll we do it?"

"Trail behind us—between those two rock slabs. Saw it when I came off the plateau to warn—"

"Warn—you mean you came down from there to warn me?" Mason broke in incredulously.

"Couldn't yell. Apaches would've cracked down on you fast then—and that would have ended it."

Mason continued to stare at Starbuck in a troubled, not-understanding way. His thin lips were set and his small eyes were dark and filled with a sullen bitterness.

"Reckon I truly am obliged to you," he muttered, almost resentfully.

"Forget it. What we've got to worry about is staying alive. Next time—"

Shawn's words were cut off abruptly as the air once again was filled with yells. A half-dozen Apaches rushed into the open, breaking from the thick brush to the south and heading for a large mound of rocks and weed-covered earth a dozen strides away.

Mason rested the old Walker on his left forearm, pressed off a shot. It was a clean miss. Starbuck, wishing he had grabbed his rifle before he turned the sorrel loose, steadied himself against the rock, dropped the buck in the lead as Mason thumbed back the hammer of his weapon, fired again. This time his aim was good. The brave spun, went down in a swirl of dust, feet beating a tattoo against the sun-baked soil. Those remaining, suddenly dissuaded, wheeled, rushed back for the shelter of the brush.

Hastily reloading, Starbuck turned his attention to Mason's bay. "What's wrong with your horse?"

He was calculating their chances for escape by making a run for it, assuming they could gain the plateau above.

"Hoofs are split. Left fore's in bad shape. Been leading him all day."

Mason could forget riding him—at least until the horse could rest and receive treatment. But the situation wasn't too serious. The sorrel could carry double. He was a big animal, stronger than average—and Mason didn't look to weigh much. The gelding, however, could not be expected to take on such a load for any lengthy distance. He'd had an ordinary day, covering quite a few miles in the intense heat, and was himself in need of rest. Again Shawn considered the trail leading up between the cleft in the rocks. It was their only hope.

"Apaches'll be trying something else pretty quick. We've got them in a stand-off right now, but they won't let it stay at that."

"Why don't they use their guns?"

"Saw only a couple in the bunch. Could be more but I doubt it—and they don't want to waste bullets. Big reason they're after us—they want our guns and ammunition."

Mason brushed at his eyes. "Was we to spot the ones with rifles, pick them off, maybe we could get past the others. Not too hard to dodge a lance."

"Would work only we don't know for sure how many've got guns. Spotted a couple, but I've got a hunch there're more braves out there, and that could mean more rifles."

"Then what—"

"They're trying to reach that pile of rocks. If they can get a couple of braves bedded down there, they can come at us from three directions. I figure we'd be smart, if we're lucky enough to turn them back their next try, to make a run for that trail, try to get on top."

"Horses'll slow us up—"

"I'll send the sorrel ahead. The bay'll follow if we do a little persuading. No sense trying to lead them—and we've got to have them if we do get there."

"Bay of mine won't be of any use. . . . You make a try for it—I'll hold them off long as I can."

15

"No need for that. Sorrel can carry double, leastwise until we're far enough to be fairly safe. Not long now until dark."

Mason brushed wearily at his sweaty face. "Glad of that. Be cooler. Heat's about got me down."

"Moving toward the desert. Days won't get any better."

And then once more the sink echoed with the piercing shrieks of Apaches. Three braves spurted from the brush, lunged for the rocky mound. They were not alone in the attempt. From the opposite side of the formation two more bucks appeared, running low, one carrying a rifle. The scheme was evident; they were endeavoring to split the fire of the men behind the rock, thereby increase the chances of the one with the rifle to gain protection of the mound.

Shawn, again bracing himself against the rock, once more cursing himself for not having his own long gun, leveled his weapon at the dodging figure with the Army Springfield, squeezed off the trigger. The Apache threw wide his arms as the slug caught him in the chest while the Springfield went spinning into the dust. He pivoted then to aid Mason. He had stopped the lead man of the trio; the two others had slowed.

"Keep 'em busy!" Shawn yelled, turning to the horses.

Grabbing the sorrel's leathers, he led the gelding to the mouth of the trail, pointed him upgrade, and slapped him sharply on the rump. As the big horse, startled, leaped away, Shawn seized the bay's reins, sent him into the cleft in quick pursuit.

Immediately he wheeled, dropped back to Mason's side. A rifle cracked. The bullet spanged into the wall of the butte behind him, screamed off into space. A wry grin on his lips he wiped sweat from his face, hunkered beside Mason. That had been a close one.

He looked toward the mound. Another of the braves had snatched the fallen rifle and was making use of it. He had reached the rocks, finding his opportunity while Starbuck was attending the horses and Mason was concentrating on the Apaches coming in from his side, was now firmly entrenched just below the crest. Only the top of his head and a small glint of the rifle were visible. More bucks were coming into the open now, weaving and dodging in and out, taking courage from the belief that shortly they would have the men behind the rock pinned down. That fact dawned swiftly on Shawn Starbuck also.

"Come on!" he yelled at Mason, and emptying his pistol at the Apaches, raced for the mouth of the trail.

3

Heaving for breath, sweat cutting channels in the dust clothing his face and neck, Shawn gained the summit of the trail. He glimpsed the horses off to one side on the plateau, mentally recorded their location as he thumbed cartridges into his weapon, and wheeled back to the edge of the plateau. Mason swung in beside him, gasping from the hard climb.

"They're coming!" he managed.

Starbuck dropped to his knees, looked down into the sink. A dozen Apaches were swarming across the sandy stretch of open ground that separated the mound of earth from the rock behind which he and Mason had stood, and racing for the mouth of the trail. Raising his pistol, he snapped a shot at the brave in the lead. The bullet, too hastily fired, missed its weaving target, but did have its effect; instantly the glistening, sweaty figures melted into the nearby brush.

"Take the horses—head that way," Shawn directed in a quick, hard voice and pointed to the path leading southward. "I'll be coming shortly."

Mason, recognizing the wisdom of the plan, moved off immediately, and catching up the trailing reins of the two mounts, started down the trail. Shawn wheeled again to the sink. The Indians were still in hiding, crouched low in the underbrush and behind the rocks.

He was not visible to them, he knew, and that alone was keeping them pinned down, since they were not anxious to brave guns positioned they knew not where. But they would throw off their reluctance, patience at such times not being one of their virtues; two or three of the bolder ones would work their way around, attempt to close in from the sides. It would require an hour at least

17

—and that was long enough to permit Mason and him to get clear of the area.

He should take full advantage of the situation, however; buy as much time as possible. Glancing about, he noticed a thick stand of wolfberry growing among a scatter of rocks at the edge of the flat. Bulling his way into its center, he drew several of the tallest stems into a sort of column. Holding them together, he removed his hat, perched it on the tips of the thorny uprights, then returned to the open ground.

Hunkered on his heels, he considered his handiwork, grunted in satisfaction. The hat had settled down to just the proper level when the stems had straightened. From the sides, the angle at which the Apaches would first view it, there would appear to be a man forted up in the rocks and brush. It was costing him a good hat—but better no headgear than no hair.

Such would further delay the renegades, and while they were figuring out a means for coping with this danger, he and Mason should be able to get well beyond their reach. But it would be wise to play it for all it was worth. Staying low, he returned to the rim of the plateau, and flat on his belly, peered down into the basin. At first he saw nothing, no signs whatever of the Apaches—and then the moving of a clump of sage drew his attention.

A smile pulled at his lips as he brushed away the sweat slipping into his eyes. The Apaches were up to an old trick —that of holding clumps of weeds or thickly leafed branches over themselves to mask their advance. Muffling the click with the cupped palm of his left hand, Starbuck thumbed back the hammer of his forty-five, kept his gaze on the brush-pocked ground at the foot of the butte.

A bush somewhat apart from the others stirred, moved forward a few inches. Shawn leveled his weapon at the clump, squeezed off a shot. The bush erupted instantly, coming apart into several sections. A lank figure leaped upright, spun, scurried for the more substantial cover of the nearby rocks.

Starbuck pulled back quickly. It wasn't necessary to see what the remaining braves, so painstakingly advancing under their camouflage, would do; they'd simply stall, debate with themselves, and shortly abandon the ruse, realizing the white men entrenched on the plateau above were onto their plan. Their next logical move would be to pull back, circle wide, and come in from opposing points, whereupon their attention would be focussed at once upon a man lying in wait for them in the brush.

18

Keeping low and well back from the rim of the butte, Shawn moved off down trail at a trot, being careful to plant his feet in the soft, yielding sand and deaden the sound of his retreat. He was already feeling the lack of the hat he'd left in the wolfberry; the sun's rays had slackened little in their ferocity although the afternoon was growing late. But darkness would soon prevail, and with it would come relief.

He saw Mason a short time later as he rounded a shoulder of granite. The older man halted at once, wheeled, faced him unsmiling.

"That shot—they come at you again?"

Starbuck took the sorrel's reins into his own hands, shook his head. "Just letting them know I was there. Longer they think they're pinned down, the better for us." Swinging onto the saddle, he kicked his foot free of the stirrup, extended his hand to Mason. "Let's go."

The man frowned, hesitated, and then as Shawn reached farther, more insistently toward him, he took the proffered arm, slid his toe into the wooden bow, and settled himself behind Starbuck.

"Can't go far in this country, riding double," he said, pulling the bay in behind the sorrel with the reins as a lead rope.

"Don't aim to—only until we're far enough from here to be safe. Other side of that hogback ought to be about right."

"That's Cibique Ridge," Mason said.

Starbuck, glancing back over the trail to be certain it was still empty and they were as yet not followed, touched the sorrel with his spurs and moved the big horse out. Apparently Mason was no stranger to the land, yet he seemed oddly reserved concerning the fact. There was a reason, he supposed, and further guessed that if Mason wanted him to know about it, he'd speak up.

"You lose your hat?"

Starbuck nodded. "Sort of. Planted it back there on the flat, in some brush."

"Tricking the Apaches?"

"Hoping to."

"Have to rig you up something before tomorrow. Man sure can't be out in this sun for long without covering up his head. Bake your brains."

"Got an old one in my saddlebags. I'll dig it out in the morning. Not much, but it'll do until I can get to where I can buy another."

They rode on in silence after that, and a time later, with

19

sunset a flaring explosion of color beyond the purple Mazatzal Mountains to the west, they pulled into a small clearing at the foot of a high palisade.

"Man never knows about Apaches," Starbuck said, staring at the dully gleaming face of the formation, all light and shadow from the cloud-reflected rays of the sun, "but I don't think they'll bother us any more tonight. If things worked like I planned, it'll be full dark by the time they learn there's nobody under that hat—and then it'll be too late to track us."

Mason nodded, slipped from his perch on the sorrel. Shawn dismounted, began to tug at the gelding's cinch buckles. Glancing at Mason, stolidly removing gear from the bay, he let his eyes run swiftly over the man's equipment. He traveled light, that was certain; no brush coat, no chaps, no slicker—only a canteen and what appeared to be totally empty saddlebags and a single wool blanket. Mason was no working cowhand, that was evident.

"That got water in it?" he asked, ducking his head at the almost new container.

"About half full," Mason replied, laying his saddle aside. The hull was old, badly cracked, with the lining of the skirt torn and missing in several patches. "Filled it this morning."

"Grub?"

"About out. Bite or two left, I reckon."

"Got plenty for the both of us," Shawn said. "Be in Lynchburg tomorrow. Can stoke up on supplies then."

"Obliged to you, but I'll get by," Mason replied, his tone making it clear he asked for no favors.

Starbuck shrugged, pulled his saddle free of the gelding, and placed it carefully on its side under a nearby clump of brush.

"Glad to share what I've got. . . . You want to work on your horse while I throw a meal together?"

Mason paused. "Not a hell of a lot I can do for him."

"Main thing you need is water—and we've got enough to get by if you use what's in your canteen."

"You mean I ought to soak his hoofs?"

"Only thing to do. Mix up some mud, then take rags, pack it around his hoofs, like a poultice. Keep things sort of wet all night and he may be in shape to ride in the morning if we take it easy."

"You think it'll help?"

"Know it will. Had the same trouble with the sorrel. Hoofs dry out, usually because some dunderheaded blacksmith gets careless with his rasp and scrapes off too much

20

of that coating—varnish, I've heard it called—when he's fitting shoes. That happens and the horse gets to traveling in country like this where it's all hot sand and never any mud, cracks open up. . . . You soak his hoofs good, then soon as you can start treating them with oil—neat's-foot or maybe linseed, whichever you can get—and you'll cure him."

Mason smiled for the first time, a brief, ragged pulling of his lips. "Guess I'd forgot that," he said, and taking the bay's reins, led him off to one side.

Shawn, staking out the sorrel, opened his saddlebags, dug out hardtack, dried beef, a can of peaches, coffee, along with a lard tin and a blackened spider. Moving to the end of the palisade, he cast a long glance to the slope, now almost wholly dark, saw no signs of the Apaches, and then crossed to the foot of the towering formation and built a small, compact fire. Placing the water-filled tin over the flames, he paused to study his companion.

Mason had given the two horses their drink, was now stirring up an amount of mud. He had produced an old undershirt, either from the flat-looking saddlebags, or perhaps utilizing the one he wore, and had ripped it into four strips.

The treatment wouldn't cure the bay's problem, but it would help. The horse should be able to make it in to Lynchburg if they took it slow and kept to soft ground. Drawing the slim-bladed Mexican knife from the sheath stitched inside his right boot, Shawn squatted, began to cut the beef into chunks, drop it into the skillet. He hesitated again as a thought came to him; he had assumed Mason was heading for Lynchburg, but in truth, he did not actually know that.

"You riding for any place in particular?" he asked, resuming his chore.

Mason was apportioning the mud onto the strip of cloth. He did not look up. "Lynchburg—then I'm going on south to the Mescal Mountain country. Got some land there."

"Was close by the Mescals once, never right down in them. Guess Lynchburg's the only town around here."

Mason nodded but made no further comment as he began to work with the bay's hooves, affixing the baglike poultices of mud, tying them securely in place while Starbuck continued his supper preparations.

The night closed in quickly and they finished the last of the coffee with only the faint glare of the fire flickering against the wall of the granite behind them to hold back

21

the shadows. Stars had broken through the flowing blackness overhead, and a pale radiance had settled over the country, softening its harshness, shrouding all things, changing them to mysterious, unfamiliar objects. Night birds began to call, timidly at first, and then more boldly; far back in the regions of the higher peaks a wolf howled, challenging one and all to dispute his dominion.

Starbuck sighed contentedly, forever moved by the matchless beauty of the night, and reaching out, picked up a handful of dry branches, tossed them into the flames.

"You born around here?" Mason wondered.

"No, Ohio's my home. Little town called Muskingum."

"What brought you west?"

"Looking for my brother. Could be you've run into him if you've done much drifting around."

"Doubt it," Mason replied listlessly.

"Be a man around twenty-five. Probably has dark hair, sharp blue eyes. Could be on the stocky side. Always sort of favored my pa in that."

"Talk like you ain't seen him in quite a spell."

"Ten years or so since he ran away from home. Pa's dead now. Need to find him so's I can clear up the estate."

"What do you call him?"

"Ben—Ben Starbuck, that's his real name, but I don't reckon he's using it. Swore he never would when he lit out that day. About all I can go on is what I think he'll look like and the fact that he's got a little scar over his left eye."

"Not much to work with."

"Found that out a long time ago. Plenty of men fit the description I give, but nobody yet has filled it."

"You think he's in Lynchburg?"

"Not exactly—maybe on a ranch nearby. I was told about a cowhand there who sort of fit the picture. Only way I ever know for sure is to do a bit of talking, have a look for that scar."

Mason was staring into the small knot of leaping flames. He opened his mouth to speak, hesitated as the wolf bayed again into the depthless night, drew this time a coyote's querulous response.

"Expect you'll maybe ride till doomsday and not find him with no more'n you've got to go on," he said finally. "This cowhand you're going to see, he got a name?"

"Jim Ivory. Ever hear of him?"

"Nope, can't say as I have. What outfit he work for?"

"Ranch called the Box C."

"Heard of it," Mason said, his tone altering. He contin-

22

ued to gaze into the fire for a time, then raising his eyes, made a motion toward the ornate, engraved belt buckle Shawn wore. "That's mighty fancy. Silver, ain't it? And that figure of a fighter on it—that ivory?"

Shawn nodded. "It was my pa's."

"He a champion fighter in that newfangled boxing style?"

"Never was a champion—a professional, but I expect he could've been, had he wanted. Nobody ever beat him."

"He learn you?"

"Taught Ben and me both. Said he wanted us to know how to take care of ourselves."

Mason stirred, wagged his head. "Sure is a wicked way for a man to fight. Once heard about a fellow mixing it up with a boxer—a professional—got himself so bad whipped folks thought somebody'd used a knife on him."

"Fists can be terrible weapons if a man knows how to use them."

"And I reckon you do."

Starbuck moved his wide shoulders slightly. "When I have to," he said, and rising, walked again to the end of the palisade where he could look back over the trail they had covered. Moon and starlight now flooded the slopes, brought all things into soft-edged focus. Nothing moved in the ethereal glow; the Apaches, he hoped, as he had hoped earlier, had given it up. Wheeling, he returned to the fire, resumed his place.

"You know," Mason said, "a thing like that could be a way to find your brother. You hear of a fighter, the boxer kind, it'd be smart to go have a look at him."

"Has brought me close a couple of times," Shawn admitted. "One of these days I'll hear about it in time, get there before the man's moved on. Need a lot of luck in what I'm trying to do."

"What you need most, seems to me," Mason said, tossing the last dregs of his coffee into the fire. "Like chasing a moonbeam. Well, reckon I'll turn in. Apaches sort of took the sand out of me. You figure we ought to stand watch?"

"No use taking chances. You go ahead, I'll take the first turn."

Mason raised no objection, simply reached for his blanket, rolled himself into it.

Starbuck's eyes were on the man curled up near the fire; he was asleep almost at once. There was something about Mason he couldn't quite fathom—something in his manner that mystified, even disturbed, him. True, he had

23

opened up a bit during the evening, become more talk-
ative, but thinking back Shawn realized the man had re-
vealed little of himself—and nothing of his past.

It was Mason's own business, he decided, again coming
to his feet. Drawing his rifle from its scabbard, he walked
slowly toward the end of the palisade and the outcrop of
rock that would provide a sentry post from which to observe the trail. A man has a right to keep his personal history to himself if so inclined. One thing sure, Mason didn't
seem too pleased by the fact they would soon be in Lynchburg.

4

They were up well before dawn, both realizing that with the coming of light came also danger from the Apaches. The night had passed without incident, but now a new day faced them and the odds were the renegades, at that very moment, were searching out the tracks of the two horses.

In a tight silence they ate hurriedly, packed their gear, and by the time the first raw sunlight was tipping the crags of the more distant ranges and flooding down the long slopes, they were mounted and on their way—Shawn wearing the battered old hat he had dug out from the bottom of his saddlebags, Mason considerably more at ease now that he was again mounted.

The mud treatment and the night's rest had done much for the bay, and while he was, of course, far from cured, some of the lameness had disappeared and he was usable. If ridden sensibly and with care, he should last out the remainder of the journey to the settlement.

All that could change swiftly, Starbuck realized. If the Apaches were trailing them and gained rapidly, thus nullifying their lead, the bay would be unable to stand any hard running even for a short distance. The alternative to a headlong race—that of forting up or once more making a stand—would be necessary. He hoped this time a more advantageous spot could be found.

Mason seemed to have improved somewhat in spirit. While the hard-cornered bleakness of his features had not vanished, there was a breaking down in the bitterness that seemed to fill him, and for the first time since they had met, there appeared to be an appreciation for the broad, savage vistas of the country through which they were slowly making their way.

Once, near mid-morning, when they halted on a long ridge to breathe the horses and probe their back trail for pursuit, he gazed out over the endless, rolling country and sighed quietly. There was a vacuity to the man, as if somewhere along the line life had dealt him a terrible blow from which he had not recovered.

"You never know how much you can miss all this—the mountains and the sky—even the heat, until it's taken away. Can miss anything, I reckon. Sounds funny maybe but a man can miss the smell of blood and death once he's grown used to it, and then puts it behind him."

Starbuck's eyes were on the distant slopes. He thought he had seen movement but wasn't certain. "Suppose so, but I wasn't in the war so I don't know. You were, I take it."

"Four years—four goddam years."

"It was hell, I'm sure of that," Starbuck said, deciding the motion he thought he saw was merely the shimmer of steadily rising heat. "I've heard others hash it over."

"Something nobody won—a man ought to remember that. Nobody ever wins a thing like that. The North came out on top but that don't mean it won. I wore a blue uniform, fought for Mr. Lincoln's idea of saving the Union. But I lost—personally. Everything except a piece of land I've got down in the Mescals. Was the same story with every man that got into it except the rich ones. They just got richer."

"Plenty of them lost, too—fortunes in cash as well as property."

"Property—land," Mason went on as if not hearing, "that's all that counts in this world. Man can lose cash, his house and furniture, cattle—things like that, and start over. But if he loses his land he's finished. He's got nothing to start from."

"This place of yours, in the Mescals. You planning to make a new start there?"

Mason turned, rubbed the bay's neck slowly. "What I aim to do. Was just getting it going when the war hit. Felt I had to go. My folks tried to talk me out of it but I was young and full of vinegar—wanted to do my part for my country. Wouldn't listen, went just the same.

"Reckon it made them kind of proud of me, being one of the few who went and volunteered from around here. Anyway, I'd just begun building my cabin—and I plain up and walked off to do my bit leaving behind five thousand acres of good grass, timber, and year-round water just standing there."

"You've never been back?"

26

Mason shook his head, lapsing again into that near sullenness that characterized him. "Not since."

Shawn moved to the sorrel, reached for the reins, and prepared to mount. Idly, he glanced once more to the trail behind them; no sign of Apaches, but his thoughts had centered on something else: the war had ended ten years ago; where had Mason been in the intervening time?

"Sounds like a fine place," he commented, going to the saddle.

"It's going to suit me," Mason said in a low voice and let the subject drop, offering no explanation as to why he had taken a decade to return to what obviously was very dear to his heart.

Starbuck waited until the man had mounted, and then led off, continuing along the ridge which lifted gradually to a higher plane where a round, thumb-like peak thrust itself bluntly into the sky.

It was all much like the land he had so recently covered in New Mexico, he thought as he swept the surrounding country with his glance. The same clean, blue sky with its batches of snowy cotton clouds; the same yellow and tan earth gashed here and there with reds and browns; the same towering hills, some clothed in green, others in barren, gray rock.

But then this had been part of New Mexico once, he recalled, before the war began. At the onset a Confederate colonel, John Baylor he thought it was, had split the territory down its center and given the western portion the name Arizona.

It had been a shrewd move on the part of the officer; those souls inhabiting that part of the sprawling domain had long sought separation and independence. For the miles that lay between them and the capital in Santa Fe were hazardous and long—so long in fact that their pleas and presence had gone practically unnoticed year after year by the politicos in power.

Mesilla, a settlement not far north of El Paso and adjacent Fort Bliss, was declared the capital of the new district, but such glory was short-lived. A victorious North, while permitting the division of the land to stand, thereby breaking up a territory that would have proved a close rival in size to Texas, voided Mesilla's claim to fame and relegated it once again to the status of irrelevancy—a small town dozing in the sun, disturbed only now and then by the noisy exploits of passing outlaws.

It was close on to noon when they reached the base of the huge peak, and there again paused to rest the horses.

27

Shawn took advantage of the opportunity to inspect the bay's hoofs, found them holding up well. Another night's rest and packing in soft mud, followed by applications of oil, and the horse would be on the way to recovery.

"He'll make it if we keep taking it easy," he said, moving to a rise on the rocky flat surrounding the peak. Gaining its highest point, he turned his gaze once more to the trail over which they had passed. He stiffened, his attention being drawn to a dozen or so figures crossing a sun swept flat in the valley below. Apaches. They had gained appreciably.

"There they are," he said, pointing.

Mason climbed to Shawn's side, followed his leveled arm. "Them sure enough. Dogging our tracks."

"Means we'll have to move faster. They'll try to cut us off and I don't know how far we are from Lynchburg."

"Ten, maybe twelve miles," Mason said readily, and pointed to another, somewhat higher ridge forming a horizon in the southeast. "Town's on the yonder side of that —in the middle of a big valley—the Rockinstraw they call it."

Again Shawn realized Mason was a great deal more familiar with the country than he let on.

"No need stewing over them getting close. We just move right along like we've been doing and we'll soon be in the Rockinstraw," Mason continued, turning back to where the horses waited. "Won't bother us there."

They pressed on shortly after that, a heavy silence, for some unaccountable reason, falling upon the two men— one that was broken only when around the middle of the afternoon, they reached the foot of the ridge's far side and were on a well-marked road leading to the settlement.

A while later they pulled off into a grove of sycamores where a small creek cut a clear, narrow channel, watered the horses and took advantage of the occasion to wash the caked dust from their faces and arms. Refreshed, and leaning against one of the trees, Starbuck stretched, yawned.

"Going to feel good sleeping in a real bed, eating somebody else's cooking for a change." Pulling off the old hat he'd produced from his saddlebags, he dusted himself down the front. "Reckon about the first thing I'd better do, however, is blow myself to a new lid. Seen better-looking hats on the plow horses back home."

Mason ignored the humor, merely nodded. "Man can miss the comforts or he can get used to doing without."

"Sure," Shawn agreed, "but when a man's been on the

28

trail for what seems like months, the change is mighty welcome."

They moved on after that and soon houses began to appear in the broad sweep of the valley; small ranches, a dirt farmer here and there, planted fields, haystacks. Still in the distance and somewhere near center, smoke was rising into the sky; Lynchburg would lie there, Starbuck guessed.

He wondered where the Box C would be, remembered then that it was to the west of the settlement some twenty miles, and shifted his attention to that direction. A faint, blue haze clung to the area and all was not as definite as it might have been. It appeared to be an area of low, rolling hills, like gray bubbles spread across a wide flat beyond which were many buttes and benches. There was no large timber visible except in the higher reaches edging the Rockinstraw to the north.

A mile short of town, which loomed up suddenly when they broke out of a thickly brushed swale onto a level flat, two men in a buggy cut in from a side road, overtook their slowly moving horses quickly, and passing by, made the customary salutary wave. Both then turned abruptly, as if startled, stared briefly, and then continued on toward the settlement at a fast clip.

Lynchburg itself looked to be slumbering in the afternoon's intense heat when Shawn and Mason turned into the single main street and proceeded slowly. Starbuck, brushing at the freshly accumulated sweat on his forehead, pointed at what evidently was the largest saloon—the Maricopa.

"Don't know about you, but a beer is the only thing that's going to cut the cotton out of my throat. What do you say we stop there first?"

"Suits me," Mason replied indifferently.

Together they swung from the street's center, rode up to the hitchrack, and dismounted. In that next moment Shawn was aware of motion directly behind them. He threw a glance over his shoulder. A man wearing the star of a town marshal pinned to the pocket of his plaid shirt and carrying a Wells-Fargo shotgun was advancing slowly. A half-dozen men, all armed, accompanied him.

Starbuck frowned, slid a look to Mason. He, also, was aware of the group, was watching them with dark, fathomless eyes. All the ease that had erased his earlier attitude had melted away, and he was again the bitter, deeply withdrawn man he had been in the blistered depths of the sink.

Stepping away from the hitchrack, Shawn pushed his

29

worn, sweat-stained old hat to the back of his head, moved along the flank of the sorrel until he stood at the gelding's hindquarters. Leaning against the horse, he considered the oncoming lawman and his supporters stoically. On the whole he respected the men who wore the star of authority and ordinarily got along well with them, but there were those who made nuisances of themselves; this one appeared to fall in that category.

"What's on your mind, Marshal?" he asked in a patient voice.

The lawman came to a halt, his eyes narrowing as his lips pulled into a tight line. He flicked Starbuck with a sharp glance, turned his attention to Mason. The other men—merchants and town elders, Shawn supposed—ranged about him, forming a half-circle. Other persons were coming now, attracted by the conflux in the street.

A tall individual standing directly behind the lawman swore, said: "By God, it *is* him!" in a strained voice, and drew his pistol. The man next him looked familiar—one of the pair who had been in the buggy.

Patient, Shawn waited in the burning sunlight while the small clouds of dust lifting from beneath the shuffling feet of the citizenry drifted aimlessly about. This was no ordinary confrontation between a small town's officialdom and unwelcome drifters being invited to move on, he realized. This was much more—and undoubtedly serious.

"Asked you a question, Marshal," he pressed firmly.

The lawman flashed him a hard glance, and cradling the shotgun, faced his companion. "All right, Mason Lynch—put your hands up!"

"Means you too, saddletramp," the tall man who had earlier drawn his pistol added, motioning at Starbuck.

The marshal threw a confirming look at Shawn, made a gesture with the shotgun. "Now—the both of you—head for jail."

5

The marshal had called his trail partner Mason Lynch. Shawn pondered that as temper stirred through him. He'd been misled, not actually lied to, perhaps, but the truth had been withheld for some reason, and that rankled him; for now he was finding himself again in the position he continually sought to avoid—that of getting involved in someone else's troubles.

Anger for this man he had helped but who had seen fit to deceive him brimmed suddenly, spilled over, spattered also the lawman.

"The hell with you, Marshal," he said in a quiet, flat voice. "I'm not going anywhere until I get some reasons."

The lawman's face colored and the shotgun in his hands came up warningly. "You being with Lynch is all the reason I need."

"For you, maybe—not for me. There some law against bumping into a man on the trail, riding with him?"

"You lay down with a dog, you'd best figure on some fleas," the marshal said, wagging the shotgun suggestively. "You coming along, or am I going to take you?"

Shawn drew himself up fully, glanced out over the threatening crowd. Half-turning, he caught Mason's eye, saw the look of helpless frustration on his bitter features, heard the plea in his voice.

"Do what he says. This whole bunch is trigger-happy. I'll try to make Huckaby believe you once we're inside."

Starbuck shrugged, moved out into the ankle-deep dust, and took his place beside Mason. One of the men in the crowd, a husky, wide-shouldered, well-dressed blond with neatly trimmed mustache and beard, stepped in behind him, shoved him roughly.

"Damned gunslinging saddlebum, coming here. We ought to—"

31

Starbuck, anger again boiling over, swung a lightning-fast right fist, caught the man full center of his belly. The blond gasped. His eyes bulged as his color changed to a pasty white. Hands clutched to his middle, he took a few faltering steps backward, sat down hard.

Huckaby whirled, shotgun once more lifted. "You try that again, I'll bend this over your head!"

The faintest smile pulled at Starbuck's lips, but there was no humor there, only a quiet self-assurance.

"Tell him, and anybody else with the same notion," he said coolly, "they'd best keep their paws off me. I don't take a roughing up from any man—including the ones who wear a star."

Huckaby kept the twin black circles of the shotgun's muzzle drifting back and forth over Starbuck and Mason Lynch.

"I'm taking that as a threat."

"Makes no difference to me. I've done nothing to get jailed for. Your reasons for doing it had better be good."

The marshal, a thin, graying man with a hook nose, full sweeping mustache, and small, black eyes that peered out from the deep sockets of a heavily veined face, nodded slowly.

"You've heard it."

"No reason far as I'm concerned."

In the tense, hot silence of the street the only sound was the retching of the man Starbuck had struck. Huckaby said: "That's because you don't know nothing. Get inside. I'll do my talking there. Rest of you people," he added, not taking his glance off his two prisoners, "clear out. I want help, I'll ask for it."

Shawn, shoulders stirring in resignation, moved on with Mason Lynch at his side. The crowd, ignoring the lawman's order, followed. As they stepped up onto the landing fronting the jail, Shawn looked back, saw several men helping the blond, still holding tight to his belly, into the Maricopa Saloon. Starbuck reckoned he shouldn't have hit the man such a punishing blow, but he'd asked for it.

"Keep your hands up," Huckaby ordered crisply, hurrying into the room behind them. "Stand over there against the wall—facing it."

Mason complied obediently. Starbuck, anger never decreasing, followed reluctantly. When he had taken his position, the lawman dropped back to the doorway.

"Homer—you and Pete Fortney, come in here. You too, Spearman. Want some witnesses." Huckaby paused, and as the men summoned thumped into the heat-packed little office, he asked the crowd in general: "How about Kemmer? He hurt bad?"

"Nope," a voice replied. "Got knocked loose from his wind—and doing some puking. Said it felt like that jasper drove a knife clean through him."

The lawman grunted. "Well, you tell him if he gets to feeling right, he's to come over here. Being on the town council, he's in this, too."

Boot heels rapped on the bare floor again as the marshal turned back into the room. Shawn felt the weight on his hip lighten as his pistol was yanked from its holster.

"Turn around."

At the lawman's command Starbuck wheeled slowly, stiffly, keeping a tight grip on himself as he faced the four men standing behind the desk at the opposite end of the sweltering office. All were sweating freely, and one, a dark-bearded, elderly man, drew out a red bandanna, mopped nervously at his neck.

"Hurry this up, Virg," he said peevishly. "I got my place to look after."

Shawn took a half-step forward, words forming on his lips, checked when he felt Mason's finger press into his arm.

"Hold off. I got you into this—let me try getting you out."

"Be none of that!" Huckaby barked. "I want you to talk, I'll tell you."

Mason's shoulders stirred with indifference. "Happens this man here's my friend—only one I've got, far as I know—and I don't aim to see him hoorawed on account of me."

Huckaby laid the shotgun across the desk where it would be within quick reach, wagged his head. Pulling off his hat, he dropped it beside the gun.

"Don't try peddling that bull to me, Lynch. I know you and I figure anybody running with you's going to be the same stripe. What are you doing here?"

The arrogance of the question was like a slap in the face to Starbuck. "This is a free country. Expect he can go anyplace he likes!"

"Don't apply to him," commented the second of the men the lawman had called in—a balding, fat man with the smell of a livery stable to him.

"Applies to everybody—"

"Nope, not to him," Huckaby persisted stubbornly, verifying the other's contention. "You giving me an answer, Lynch?"

33

Mason said: "Came back for some things I've got stored away, left with some folks."

"What folks?"

"The Schmitts. A trunk of family things, keepsakes and the like."

"Heine Schmitt's place burnt down five year ago," Homer said. "Him and his missus were lost in the fire along with everything else inside the house."

Mason Lynch's head came up slowly as if in disbelief. The livery-stable man clawed at his chin. Beyond the doorway in the street a voice reported loudly: "Claims he come back to see old Heine Schmitt—"

"You'd best come up with a better answer'n that," Huckaby said drily.

"Only one I've got," Mason said in a weary tone. "The truth."

"Then there ain't no reason why you can't climb back on your horse and move on," the lawman said with finality. "The both of you."

"Don't count on me," Starbuck drawled, pushed as far as he intended to be. "I came here on some personal business, and I intend to see it through. I wind it up, I'll ride out. Now, that'd better suit you, Marshal, because that's the way it's going to be."

Huckaby's face colored darkly. Homer glanced at him, then at the pair with him. He wagged his head in dissatisfaction. "I don't like this, Virg—not a damned bit. Them two are up to something. They've got no call coming back here except to even up that score."

"Whatever that means—it's wrong," Shawn snapped. "Business I've got here is with a man working on a ranch called the Box C. Don't figure that it's any of your put-in, but a stranger seems to need a reason for coming to your town."

The room was in complete silence. Finally Huckaby spoke. "You say the Box C?"

"Got nothing to do with the Canfields and the trouble I had with them," Mason said hurriedly. "My friend here is named Starbuck, and he's looking for his brother. Thinks maybe one of the hands out there could be him."

Homer looked in scorn at the others, centered his attention on the lawman. "Man'd sure have to be mighty goddam dumb to swallow a yarn like that! Just happens to be going to see a cowboy who's working for the Canfields—the brothers of the man his partner Lynch here spent ten years in the pen for killing! Any fool can see what they've got in mind."

Shawn stared at Mason. The puzzling things concerning the man were making some sense now; the gap of years that had elapsed since the war's end, the deep-seated bitterness, the desperate but reluctant hopefulness overshadowed by some deep fear.

Mason felt the pressure of Starbuck's thrusting gaze. "Guess I should've told you—explained—"

"Something I'd best do—want him to get it straight," Huckaby broke in, his manner toward Shawn relenting somewhat as it became apparent to him that he was making a mistake insofar as the tall rider was concerned. "This fellow you took up with on the trail is Mason Lynch. Born about twenty miles west of here—on the ranch you're talking about, the Box C. Only then it belonged to his folks and was just called the Lynch place. His pa and ma were the first people to settle here in the valley—that's why the town's named Lynchburg, after them. He tell you that?"

"Some of it," Starbuck replied, not wanting to make it any worse for Mason than it already was. But within him there was a smoldering resentment for the man; he had been a friend—Mason had not returned that friendship, had instead permitted him to become a part of his trouble, whatever it was.

"Before the war started everything was going along everyday like. Then Mason went off and when he came back four years later, he found his folks had died, and that they'd sold off their place to the Canfield brothers. Deal was made a few months before they passed on—a runaway accident. They'd been living right here in town, in Homer Boyd's hotel."

"Nobody'll ever make me believe they just up and sold out," Mason said in a low, dogged voice.

Virg Huckaby slapped the top of his desk in exasperation. "Goddammit—that's what got you in trouble before! They sold—and the Canfields have got the papers to show it."

"Anybody around here see my pa sign them papers? You see him do it, Marshal? Names can be forged."

"Wasn't nothing like that happened. Deal was all straight and legal, even if it wasn't made right under your nose. Anyway," Huckaby said, coming back to Shawn, "Mason here got all worked up and jumped Wade Canfield—there was three of the brothers—and they both went for their irons. Mason was a mite quicker, killed Wade. I barely got him out of town and hid before Kit

35

and Barney Canfield, and a bunch of their hired hands and friends, could get to him to string him up.

"Finally got him to a trial and the judge was right generous to him—because he'd been a soldier, I suspect. Gave him ten years in the pen instead of hanging him or putting him away for life, way most folks figured he ought've done."

Shawn Starbuck had listened in silence. It was not a new story, simply a variation of the old one; a man makes a mistake, pays for it—but there are those who will never let him forget. Unconsciously, his sympathies drifted to Mason.

"Most folks," Starbuck repeated the words carefully. "That include everybody besides the Canfields and their friends?"

Huckaby bristled slightly. "Most folks—just leave it at that," he said.

Mason stirred. "Reckon you can see now why they ain't exactly happy to see me around here."

Shawn nodded. "Think you've come back to kill off the rest of the Canfields—cause a lot of trouble for everybody."

"Only that's not it at all. I aim to move on. What I said was the truth—I left a trunk full of family belongings with the Schmitts. They say it got burned up so I've got no reason to hang around. I'm ready to ride on—"

"Except you're not going anywhere until that horse of yours gets some doctoring."

"The bay? What's the matter with him?" the livery-stable owner asked, looking through the dust-filmed window.

"Dry hoofs. Starting to split. Left front's pretty bad. I packed them in mud last night but having to ride him today sort of undid all the good. Needs more rest and doctoring."

The lawman swung to the stocky stable owner. "That right, Pete?"

"Can't tell from listening—have to look him over. Splitting sure can cripple a horse. But he was rode in and I don't recollect him being too lame. Expect, was I to work on him, he could be in shape tomorrow."

"Make it noon," Starbuck said, "and we'll both ride out. I'll have my business done with by then—and I sure don't want to hang around this town any longer'n I have to."

Huckaby's features darkened and his mouth tightened. "No need to get all het up now, friend. Only natural we'd be suspicious of Mason, showing up here like he has. And

36

you riding along with him—how was we to know you wasn't some hired gun he brought along to help out?"

"Same way that I know you're not Santy Claus," Starbuck answered, his voice sharp. "One thing the bunch of you could learn—don't go jumping to conclusions the first time you see a man. Could get yourself hurt bad one of these days." He paused, faced the lawman squarely. "It's settled?"

"It's settled," Huckaby replied. "You got till noon tomorrow. Long as you don't start trouble, you won't be bothered by me."

"Supposing somebody else starts it?"

"Don't let them. Walk off. I can't be responsible for what a lot of folks've got stuck in their craw, and if you think—"

"Virg," Homer Boyd cut in, staring through the open doorway into the street, "maybe you'd best hold up on that there agreement you're making. Here comes the Canfields. Kit and Barney both. Could be they might not go for it."

6

A splintery light came into Huckaby's black eyes and the corners of his mouth pulled down to hard lines. Mason Lynch shifted nervously.

"I'll be taking my gun back, Marshal."

"The hell you will," he said in a tightly controlled voice. "I'm the law around here—not the Canfields."

Horses pounded up to the hitchrack fronting the jail, halted. A babble of words sounded in the street and then boot heels rapped a quick, angry cadence on the pine landing. Shortly a ruddy-faced redhead with snapping blue eyes came through the doorway, followed by a larger, dark-haired man. The Canfields sure didn't look much alike, Shawn thought.

The redhead shot a hasty glance around the room, planted himself squarely before Mason Lynch. Lower jaw outthrust, hands on hips, he said: "You've got a hell of a lot of gall coming back here!"

"Ease off, Kit," Huckaby said stiffly. "Reckon he's got a right to—"

"No he ain't! Got no rights at all around here, far as I'm concerned! The sonofabitch lost them when he murdered Wade!"

"Went to the pen for that," Mason said woodenly. "Cost me ten years out of my life."

"Should've been hung!" Canfield snapped, whirling to Huckaby. "I want him out of here, Virg!"

The lawman's anger blazed instantly. "*You* want him out of here! Where do you get off giving orders like that? I'm the marshal here—not you."

The rancher's eyes squeezed down to narrow slots. "You heard me, Huckaby. I want him run out of town— clean out of the county, in fact—now!" He hesitated, again swept the men in the tension-filled office with his brittle glare. "You don't—then by God, I will!"

"No," Huckaby said, plainly struggling to remain calm, suppress the anger that was ripping through him, "you won't do nothing! You hear me, Kit? I won't stand for you horning in!"

Canfield threw a glance to his closemouthed brother, Barney, looked beyond him to the crowd packed around the doorway looking in, avidly absorbing the controversy. A smirk crossed the rancher's face. He settled back on his heels in a satisfied sort of way, bucked his head at Huckaby.

"You forgetting who you're talking to?"

"No—it's you who's doing the forgetting—that I'm the law around here."

"Maybe not for much longer."

The marshal drew himself up to his full height. "Meaning you'll get my job. . . ."

Canfield's eyes shifted to the three men standing behind the desk, touched each with a warning definite as if it had been put into words: this was a matter in which they were not to meddle.

"Could say that. I recollect your appointment comes up again in a couple of months. Might just be the town could stand a change."

Huckaby's expression did not alter. "Been the law around here since before you come. Like as not I'll still be after you're gone."

"Don't bet on it," the rancher said, and, turning his back on the marshal, faced Mason. "Mount up!"

"Tomorrow," Lynch said, shaking his head. "Be gone by noon."

"Hell with that. I want you out of here now."

"He stays till noon, if he's of a mind," Huckaby said. "He has my permission."

"Permission—hell . . ."

"He can't leave, Mr. Canfield," Boyd interrupted, evidently feeling pressed to ignore the rancher's visual warning. "He's got a lame horse. Pete Fortney's aiming to work on him tonight. That's the reason Virg's letting him stay."

Kit Canfield wagged his head stubbornly. "I don't give a goddam for his reasons—his or anybody else's. I want him gone!"

Starbuck, silent through the exchange, shifted angrily, unable to restrain himself any longer. "Back off, Canfield," he said, folding his arms across his chest. "The man's paid for his mistake. You've got no call riding him."

Canfield shot a quick look at Shawn, his pale eyes sparking as he took in the well-worn trail clothing, the ragged, soiled hat. His lip curled back in disdain.

"Best you keep your snoot out of this—unless you're looking for trouble."

"Which maybe I am," Shawn said mildly.

Canfield's ruddy face darkened. "Who the hell are you, anyway?"

"Friend of Mason's. Like you've been told, we're pulling out tomorrow, come noon."

"Not good enough!" Canfield declared stubbornly. "I want him gone by sundown—and if he ain't—"

Barney Canfield reached out, laid a restraining hand on his brother's shoulder. "Simmer down, Kit. Tomorrow'll be all right. He ain't about to try anything."

The redhead threw the hand off impatiently. "How do you know he ain't?" He hesitated, as if struck by the thought, pivoted to Huckaby. "I'm asking you that, Mister Marshal. How do you know he ain't here to bushwhack me and Barney like he did Wade? You tell me how?"

The lawman's mouth tightened. "Man tells me he won't, I take his word."

"Word!" Kit Canfield exploded. "You mean you'd take the word of a goddam killer? What's the law coming to in this town?" he asked, turning to Fortney and the others. "I'm mighty sure we're needing a change when the man we've got wearing the star sides with a murderer against decent folks."

"I'm not taking sides," Huckaby said quietly. "You're twisting things around to suit yourself. Like Starbuck there said, Lynch's paid for that he's done, got a right to do what he likes long as he hurts nobody."

"Well, that ain't the way I see it!" Kit shouted, again knocking aside Barney's hand. "I'm serving notice on you right now, if you don't get him out of town by dark, I'm taking things into my own hands, doing it myself."

Fortney cast an alarmed look at Homer Boyd, the hotel owner. Spearman, the third man, who had stood by the entire time in stony silence, suddenly came to life.

"Now, Mr. Canfield, we can't go doing something that'll upset—"

"Upset—hell! What if it'd been your brother he shot down?"

"That was ten years ago," Huckaby said, gaining confidence from the support he appeared to be getting. "About time you forgot it. I gave Lynch and his friend permission to hang around until noon tomorrow—mostly because there's

40

not much else they can do. I'm standing by it—and you're not to come busting into town later with a bunch of your hired hands and trying to change it. You do and I'll get word to the United States Marshal in Tucson."

"He's right, Kit," Barney Canfield murmured. "We don't want no more killings. If Huckaby's willing to stick his neck out, guarantee we'll have no trouble from Lynch, I don't see nothing wrong with letting things slide till tomorrow noon. If he ain't gone by then—well, I figure we've got us a call coming."

"Be smarter to do something about it right now," Kit Canfield muttered. Sullen, he faced Huckaby. "All right, go ahead and do it your way, but you damn well better keep them locked up tight until its time for them to travel—"

"Not much you don't lock us up!" Starbuck said, coming into the conversation. "We've done nothing to get jailed for—and we're sure not sitting out the next eighteen hours in a cell just to please you."

The rancher spun to Shawn. "Goddam you—told you to keep your nose out of things that ain't none of your business!"

"Getting locked up in a cell for nothing is my business, and it'll take more than you—"

Canfield's hand swept down to the gun at his hip, checked abruptly as Huckaby caught up the double-barreled shotgun from his desk, brought it to bear on him.

"Figured it'd come to that," the lawman said in a low voice. "When you don't get your way, you try taking it. Now, best thing for everybody is for you to get out of town, and stay out. Forget about Lynch and Starbuck. I'll see to them."

Kit Canfield swore angrily, glared at Mason, who returned his stare with unblinking eyes.

"Huckaby's right," Barney said, taking a firm grip on his brother's arm this time. "Be smart to pull out, leave it up to him. It goes wrong, it'll be him we'll blame."

The redhead nodded slowly, seemingly calm now. "I'll do more than blame him," he said in a promising sort of tone, "I'll make him sorry he ever pinned on that badge!" Wheeling, he strode to the doorway, a rigid, outraged figure teetering on the edge of total violence, and halting, leveled a finger at the marshal.

"I'm not agreeing to this—want you to remember that. I'm just going along with you and them gutless bleeding hearts there behind you because Barney wants me to. Either one of us gets bushwhacked, I—"

"Ain't nobody going to get hurt—"

"You willing to guarantee that?"

The lawman, with the hating look of a man pushed to the wall, nodded impatiently. "All right, I'm guaranteeing it!"

Kit Canfield spat into the dust beyond the doorway, nodded abruptly, and with Barney at his heels, stepped out onto the landing. Immediately there was a flurry of questions from the bystanders in the street, all of which were ignored, and then the Canfields were mounted and spurring away.

For a time the men in the lawman's cramped quarters were still, and there were only the sounds from the street —the muffled words of those loafing about the front of the building, the more distant noises of the town's normal activities. Finally Pete Fortney heaved his bulk away from the wall against which he had been leaning, and rubbing his sweaty palms together in a nervous way, started for the door.

"Expect I'd better get that horse over to my place, start working on him. Sure don't want that to be the reason you can't leave tomorrow, Mason."

Boyd scratched at his beard, equally shaken. "God, no! Don't let nothing mess things up. If I know Kit, he'll do what he's threatening to."

Turned edgy by the words Canfield had whipped him with, Huckaby spun to the hotel man. "You saying I can't keep him or anybody else in line around here?"

"Not saying no such a damn thing! Only—"

Starbuck stepped into the sudden breech that could lead to more wrangling. "Be obliged if you'll take my sorrel along with the bay," he said to Fortney. "Give him a measure of grain along with the hay. Better watch the water—and I'd be obliged if you could find time to rub him down."

"Got the time," the stableman rumbled. "Two hostlers laying around the place most of the day, doing pure nothing. What about your gear?"

"Leave my saddlebags at the hotel when you go by. Aim to put up there for the night."

The tension in the heat-filled room had cleared. Fortney went through the doorway, muttered something to the crowd outside, crossed the street and took charge of the two horses. Homer Boyd and the tight-mouthed Spearman followed immediately, separating as they stepped into the open. Shawn looked questioningly at the lawman.

"We free to go?"

For a reply Virg Huckaby, his expression blank, slid Starbuck's pistol across the desk to him. Mason extended his hand. The marshal shook his head.

"Be getting yours back when you're ready to ride out. And I'm putting Starbuck in charge of you."

"Now, hold on!" Lynch protested. "That ain't right, you loading me onto his back. Doubt he'll want to be bothered anyhow."

"Said he was your friend, didn't you?"

"Sure, but that was before—"

Shawn stirred, wiped at the sweat on his face. "It's all right. I'm owning up to being considerable put-out at the way you kept me in the dark, but it's over and done with. Best thing we can do is forget it."

"Reckon I did look at it wrong, but I couldn't see no reason for telling you my troubles—not after what you done for me back there in that sink."

"What was that?" Huckaby asked, watching the two move for the doorway.

"Apaches. Had me cold. Starbuck saved my hide."

Huckaby nodded, thought for a moment. "Good. Then you ain't likely to cross him up, do something foolish."

"Not about to," Lynch replied soberly. "I ain't so stocked up with friends that I can afford to lose even one."

Again the lawman signified his approval. "See that you keep thinking that way. And watch your step, the both of you. Where you headed now?"

"After that beer we were thirsting for when you and that reception committee stopped us," Shawn said.

"Then you're going to the hotel—"

"Going to find ourselves a square meal first. Both a might gaunt."

"Try Ma Chuckson's. Grub's real good there. What about that personal business you mentioned? When you taking care of it?"

"Figured to ride out to the Box C first thing in the morning."

"And get your head blowed off," the lawman said sarcastically. "You loco or something?"

Starbuck scratched at the stubble on his jaw. He hadn't given that side of it much thought, being anxious to meet with Jim Ivory, but since the Canfields seemed to think he was a close friend of Mason Lynch's, possibly even a hired gun, it would be stupid just to go riding in. But it was an errand that had to be completed—the reason, in fact, that he was there. He shrugged.

"Have to manage it somehow."

43

"Best thing'll be for me to ride with you," Huckaby said. "Me and the Canfields don't see eye to eye on much of anything, but they ain't apt to try nothing with me along."

Starbuck agreed. "Be obliged to you. How about a beer with us?"

"Maybe later, thanks," the marshal said, and then as Shawn and Mason Lynch stepped out into the street, added, "You watch yourselves. Don't want no trouble."

"No trouble," Starbuck assured him, and with Mason at his side, walked through the few remaining onlookers yet gathered in front of the jail and crossed to the saloon.

7

Hostility, like a dark and solid mass, met them as they pushed through the saloon's swinging doors and halted in the smoke-filtered lamplight. The silence was abrupt, and as Shawn and Mason angled for the bar extending along the opposite wall, two men lounging against it took up their drinks, sauntered off into the scatter of tables and chairs to their right.

Starbuck, his sardonic eyes probing the large room, settled his attention on what appeared to be a congregation near center. He saw it was the man who had earlier pushed him and that he had subsequently dissuaded from further participation in the affair with a blow to the belly. Kemmer, Virg Huckaby had called him. Shawn remembered then: THE MARICOPA SALOON . . . FRED KEMMER, PROP., the sign outside had proclaimed. The man he'd slugged was the owner of the place. He gave Mason Lynch a wry grin.

"Seems I flattened the proprietor. You reckon our money'll be any good here?"

"Maybe not," Lynch replied as they halted at the long counter. "Not the only place in town."

But a moment later a balding man wearing an apron separated from a knot of sympathizers gathered around Kemmer, and moved in behind the bar.

"Beer," Shawn said, holding up two fingers.

The bartender drew two large mugs of the foaming brew, slid them across the counter. Starbuck passed a coin to the man, said, "Hold the change. We'll be wanting more," and followed Mason to a nearby table, where both sat down.

"Feels good," he said, sighing gratefully. "Tail of mine was beginning to grow to the saddle."

"Same here," Mason replied in a preoccupied sort of

45

way. He took a long swallow of his drink, set the glass back on the table. "Don't blame you for getting riled some at me. Reckon you'd like to hear some explaining now."

Starbuck shrugged, swished the amber liquid about in the container he was holding. "Little late," he said indifferently. "No surprises left. Don't bother if you're not of a mind."

Lynch bobbed his head. "Expect that's it—I want to. Nobody ever much listened to my side of the thing."

"That judge must have. Man's usually hung or sent to the pen for life when he kills somebody. Was something in your favor or it wouldn't have worked out that way. . . . You did kill Wade Canfield, didn't you?"

"Never denied that. Plenty of witnesses saw me. We were talking—was right out there in the street, in front of Gabaldon's Feed Store—about this thing of my pa selling out the place to him and his brothers.

"I was just back from the war feeling plenty busted down and out of everything. Then I was hit with the news of my folks being dead and the ranch being sold only a little while to the Canfields. Didn't make sense to me, and I told Canfield that. He didn't like the way I said it, I guess, and real quick got all fired up. He was a hotheaded one, like Kit. Next thing I knew I'd called him a liar. He went for his gun—I beat him to it. Was a dozen men who saw it."

"Long as he drew, seems more a fair fight to me."

"Only Wade Canfield was big shucks around here. Him and his brothers had brought a lot of money into the country and the town was doing right well from Canfield business. Me, the way they looked at it, brought nothing but trouble. Only natural they stood by the Canfields."

"Huckaby—seems I remember him saying he was the marshal here then, that right?"

"Virg's been marshal ever since I can recollect. Why?"

"He side with the townspeople and the Canfields?"

"About all I can say is that he seen to it that I didn't get lynched and that I got a trial."

Starbuck stared into his glass. The animosity that existed between the lawman and the Canfields was a definite force. It evidently had a basis other than Mason's trouble with the three brothers.

"But that judge was a squareshooter," Lynch went on. "Guess he sort of figured I had a break coming, sentenced me to only ten years." He hesitated thoughtfully, added: "Ten years—that's a hell of a long time."

Shawn took another swallow of beer. Some of the weariness had slipped from his long frame now as he sat in the cool depths of the shadowy saloon talking with Mason Lynch, hearing the voices of other men, savoring the odors of spilled liquor, sweat and dust, that were somehow agreeable.

"Your coming back here—it for the reason you say?"

"That's it. Wanted to pick up the stuff I'd left with the Schmitts." Lynch straightened slowly, eyes fixed upon Shawn. "You think I'm lying?"

"Not that, but since we're hashing this out I just want to get it all straight."

"You've got the truth. If my horse was able, I'd ride on right now. Got no more use for this bastard of a town than it has for me."

"Seen friendlier places," Starbuck murmured. "You still think the Canfields crooked your folks out of their ranch?"

"Thought about it a lot when I was laying it out in the pen. Still not convinced they sold—willingly, anyway—and I never will be."

"But you had a place of your own down in the Mescals and they knew you wouldn't be taking over their land when you came back. Makes sense to me they'd sell when they got the chance."

"Told myself that, and maybe down deep I believe it. But something won't let me admit it."

Shawn stirred. "You figure you're right, you ought to fight about it—only not with a gun. Get yourself a lawyer, let him dig into it. If there's been some crooking done, he'll find it."

"Mighty sure he would. Like—for one thing—where'd the money go? If the Canfield's paid the folks in cash, what happened to it? Nobody's ever been able to answer that, and there was so much dust got kicked up when I got hauled in for shooting Wade that it was lost in the shuffle."

Lynch settled back in his chair, moved his shoulders indifferently. "What the hell—I don't care now, anyway. It's all over and done with. The Canfields can have the damned place—and if I never set foot in this town again it'll still be too soon."

"Grew up here, didn't you?"

"Sure—"

"Little hard to forget that."

"Not for me—not when everybody figures you for a sonofabitch."

47

"Such a thing as a man coming back, facing up to what he's brought on himself, and living it down."

"Not worth it, far as I'm concerned. I'm going to crawl into my place in the Mescals and stay there. Be damned few times when I'll be visiting what folks call civilization because I aim to go only when starvation or something like that forces me to. I'm plumb sick of people and what they think and the million stinking laws they want a man to live by."

"There's only ten—the Commandments," Starbuck murmured. "Once heard a preacher point that out. All the rest, he said, were just little two-bit rules that men have added to the book and could be forgotten if a fellow would stick to the others."

Mason Lynch was silent for a time, then spoke again. "Reckon he's right, but it don't matter much to me now. All I want is to get off to myself, be left alone—see if I can learn to live again like a human's supposed to. In ten years a man can get out of practice."

Starbuck picked up the empty glasses, stepped to the bar and obtained refills. Setting them on the table, he resumed his chair, noting as he did that the crowd in the saloon was increasing steadily as the evening wore on.

"Being alone's not going to help much," he said after a bit. "There nobody waiting for you—a girl, maybe?"

"Was one," Mason said heavily. "If I hadn't of wound up in the pen we'd likely have married. Doubt if she's around now—and if she is, she'd be married and have herself a passel of kids."

"Never know about women. Wouldn't hurt to look her up."

A frown drew Mason's brows together. "You think—after ten years she might—"

"Like I said, women are hard to figure."

Lynch dropped his eyes. "No, not much chance of that," he said disconsolately. "But I reckon it wouldn't hurt to ask about her. Aim to go out to Ma and Pa's graves, too. Can do it all in the morning when you're seeing this Jim Ivory fellow. Good thing you've got the marshal going with you. Them Canfields'd never let you get off the place alive."

"Not so sure the marshal will get any better welcome than I will. Seems to be plenty of fire between him and Kit."

"Got the same idea. Canfields are pretty strong around here now, got the say-so, more or less, as to who'll wear

48

that star, and they figure Virg Huckaby ought to be kow-towing to them."

"Only he doesn't see it that way. Look on his face when Kit made that threat was pure hate. Speaking of looks, Kit and Barney sure don't favor each other. This Wade, the one you tangled with, he look like either one of them or was he something different yet?"

"Him and Kit are alike—both redheads. Barney's no blood kin—a stepbrother."

"What about those three the marshal called in?" Shawn continued. "You know them from away back or are they johnny-come-latelys?"

"Pete—Pete Forney, he's the stable owner, I know him. And Homer Boyd, the one with the black beard. He runs the hotel—the Mogollon. One he called Spearman is a stranger to me. Sign down the street says he runs a saddle and gun shop."

"How about Kemmer, owner of this place?"

"He was the bartender when I was last in here—ten years or so ago. Don't know what happened to Tom Keuhne. Like my folks and the Schmitts, he was one of the old bunch. Some've died off and there's a few I guess who've moved on where they can maybe make a better living. Why?"

"Always like to get things squared away in my head so if trouble pops up I sort of know who I can figure will do what."

"If it does, don't look for help from anybody around here. Whole bunch'll be looking out for themselves."

"Reckon that's normal," Shawn drawled, stretching his long legs and sighing comfortably. "Folks sort of lean to looking out for themselves, especially if they've invested a lifetime getting where they are."

"You think Virg Huckaby's that way, too?"

"Can't quite make up my mind about him. Got a tough job trying to keep the peace and still make everybody happy. Always somebody with an ax to grind putting the heat on a lawman."

"Like Canfield was doing today."

"Yeh . . . and all the time he was standing there buck-ing Kit Canfield he knew the merchants would probably line up with him and his brother if it ever comes to a real showdown."

"Kind of surprised me—him bellying up to Kit the way he done."

"Didn't have a choice if that star means anything to him. Figured once he let the Canfields grab the hoe han-

49

dle, he'd be walking on his knees to them from that minute on."

"Lot of hate inside Virg Huckaby for Kit," Mason said thoughtfully. "Like to know what caused it—but then Kit's the kind that's easy to hate, always causing trouble—"

"Which I reckon's on the way now," Starbuck cut in lazily and nodded at the Maricopa's entrance.

The Canfield brothers had just entered and halted in front of the batwings. Kit, jaw outthrust, swept the saloon with his arrogant glance. Locating Shawn and Mason Lynch, he said something over his shoulder to Barney, and then the two started forward.

Both Canfields had been drinking, Starbuck observed, but they were far from drunk as the pair swaggered up to the table. Kit stopped in front of Mason Lynch. Barney Canfield was a stride or so behind him.

"Get out, jailbird," the redhead said, jerking his thumb at the doorway. "You're leaving town."

Mason did not stir as the racket inside the saloon died rapidly. Shawn, tension building suddenly within him, drew himself up in his chair, draped one arm over the back.

"Move on, Canfield," he said softly. "We don't want trouble."

"Asked for it the minute you rode into town," the rancher countered. Swinging half around, he touched the saloon patrons with his glance as if inviting all present to hear and bear witness. "Changed my mind about the two of you—you're pulling out."

"No, I reckon not," Starbuck said. "We made a deal with the marshal, and you agreed to it—"

"Huckaby made you a deal, not me! Told everybody plain I thought it was a fool thing to do."

"You agreed, just the same—"

"The hell I did!" he shouted, wiping flecks of saliva from his mouth. "Was Huckaby and you in on it. I just went along. Got to studying on it, knew I was right, so I come back to straighten it out."

Canfield's raised voice was a powerful magnet drawing the crowd in nearer. Men began to line up along the polished counter; others continued the string into a half-circle that enclosed the Canfields and the two men at the table. The bartender, joined now by a recovered Fred Kemmer, had changed his position, stood now at the near end where he would miss nothing.

51

Shawn wagged his head slowly. There was a coolness to him, a quiet, unruffled veneer on the surface, but underneath all was boiling turbulence, crystallizing steadily into the hard-core anger men such as Kit Canfield always created within him.

"No matter how you brand it," he said, "you're backing out—welching—not standing by your word."

Canfield's red-lidded eyes flared. "Don't you go lecturing me, you goddam saddlebum!"

"Somebody ought to. Leastwise, somebody ought to teach you that a man's only as good as his word. Now Mason couldn't leave here if he was willing. Horse of his can't be ridden. You know that."

"You're goddam right I know it—and I fixed it! I'm giving you a horse, Lynch. Trading you a sound animal for that bonerack you're forking. No reason now why you can't move on."

A rueful smile crossed Mason's face. "Expect that's just what you're hoping I'll do—light out on a Box C horse. Wouldn't get five miles before you'd be coming to string me up for a horse thief."

"You'll get a bill of sale," Barney Canfield said, breaking his silence. "It's an honest offer—and better'n you deserve."

Starbuck came up stiff in his chair, irritated by the statement. "Why's that? Why is it more than he deserves? Way I see it his debt to you has been wiped out. He paid what the law said he owed for doing what he did. Come to think about it, maybe it's the other way around—maybe you owe him something. So why would trading him horse for horse be more than he deserves?"

The Canfields stared at Shawn, a puzzled look on their slack faces. His words were over their heads and completely beyond understanding. A man at the bar said something in a low breath and the one next him laughed. Kit Canfield's eyes flashed with anger and his face darkened. He flung a furious glance in that direction, rocked forward toward Shawn, began to jab at him with a forefinger.

"I don't know what the hell you're talking about, buddy," he snarled, "but whatever it is, I don't like it! Now, you and that yellow-bellied killer sidekick of yours harness yourself up and be on your way inside thirty minutes or, by God, I'll—"

The anger within Shawn Starbuck surfaced. He came to his feet in a smooth, deceptively fast motion, knocked the rancher's hand aside. The points of his jaw showed white

52

through his short stubble of beard and a hard glitter filled his eyes. He had tried to avoid trouble—but a man can take only so much.

"No need waiting, Canfield—you can start the ball right now. We're not leaving until tomorrow."

"The hell you ain't!" Canfield yelled, and swung a looping right at Starbuck's head.

Shawn blocked the blow easily with his left forearm—remembered suddenly that he had in plain words promised Virg Huckaby that he'd sidestep trouble—and catching the rancher by the shoulders, threw him back into the crowd.

"Go on home, Canfield," he said. "I don't want to fight you."

"You're sure as hell going to anyway!" Canfield shouted, beside himself with rage, and lunged.

Starbuck stepped quickly away from the table and chairs, wanting no encumbrances underfoot. He could hear the crowd yelling encouragement to the rancher, and there was a steady swishing of the batwings as more onlookers poured in from the street.

"Give him a lick or two for me, Kit!" Fred Kemmer called from behind the bar. "I'm owing him."

Canfield rushed in. Wheeling fast, Shawn halted him with a stiff left that spun the man half around. As Canfield struggled to regain his balance, Starbuck stung him sharply with several jabs to the face, crossed with a right that smacked loudly, and then danced away.

The rancher, hands dangling loosely at his sides, looked about stupidly as if not certain what had happened. The hard blows had fallen swiftly, seemingly from nowhere. He continued to hang motionless, as if listening to the yelling of the crowd, and then Barney Canfield stepped in, swung him around to where he could see Starbuck waiting patiently.

Shaking his head to clear away the webs, Canfield shuffled forward, his boots making dry, scraping sounds on the bare floor. Abruptly he swore, lowered his shoulders, charged.

"Goddam you!" he shouted, boring in with both arms flailing.

Shawn gave way before the furious rush, taking several retreating steps. He felt hands against his shoulders, realized he had backed into the crowd—into someone.

"Here he is, Kit!" Barney Canfield said, and pushed.

Starbuck stumbled forward, went head-on into a hail of rocklike fists. He weathered the onslaught, danced aside, feeling the sting and throb where the rancher's knuckles

53

had smashed into him. He tossed a side glance to Barney Canfield, regarded him with a grim, promising smile, and then squared away to meet the encouraged redhead rushing in once more.

"One of them fancy dans!" a voice cried as Shawn dropped into a stance. "Look at the way he's holding his fists!"

"Show him how a real man fights, Kit!" another added.

Canfield slowed, shuffled to a halt, smirking broadly as he regarded Starbuck. "One of them show kind, eh? Always did want to try my luck."

"Now's your chance," Shawn murmured, and flicked the rancher lightly across the eyes.

Canfield bellowed, plunged forward. Starbuck feinted, shifted fast, crossed with a right that brought Kit to a flat-footed halt. Smooth and quick, Starbuck cut back, stabbed a straight left into the rancher's face. A trickle of red began to flow from Canfield's nose. Not delaying, Shawn struck again, this time with a right that thudded.

The blow was too high on Canfield's head to do any great amount of damage, only caused him to blink, take a staggering step sideways. Starbuck, weaving, dodging, shifted to the man's right watching for another opening.

From the tail of his eye he saw motion, ducked away, spun. Barney Canfield was stepping in behind him once again. At the same instant Mason Lynch yelled a warning to that effect, Shawn came full around, unleashed a cocked fist. It caught the dark-haired Canfield on the ear, sent him sprawling to the floor.

"Stay there, damn you," Starbuck muttered through clenched teeth and wheeled to face the brother.

The rancher had taken advantage of the interruption. He was closing in fast. Shawn rocked back on his heels as a fist drove into his midsection, winced when a knotted fist grazed his jaw. Sucking for wind, he instinctively dropped low, getting beneath the pistonlike action of the man's arms, pivoted on a heel and spun away. Before Canfield could adjust to the swift change, Starbuck wheeled again, bobbed to the side, and came in, his left jabbing viciously, right shaped into a lump hard as granite, poised like a rattlesnake waiting to strike. Abruptly he found the opening.

The streaking blow found the point of Canfield's jaw. The rancher's head flew back, his arms dropped limply to his sides. Eyes rolling wildly, he staggered to one side, halted. Strength deserted him. He sank to his knees, braced himself with extended arms to prevent complete collapse.

Shouts came from the crowd, urgent cries to get up, to finish the fight, show the fancy dan. Shawn, sweat pouring off his face, waited. He slid a glance to Barney Canfield, half expecting him to make some sort of move. The younger Canfield, hand clapped to his ear, seemed content only to watch.

Kit Canfield shook his head, pulled himself laboriously to an unsteady, upright position. Rubbing at his eyes, he turned about, faced Shawn. As their glances locked, the rancher's slack jaw tightened, his arms came up with great effort, and he stumbled forward, game but almost out on his feet.

Starbuck dropped his guard, moved away, permitted the rancher to reel by. Commotion in the crowd drew his attention. Looking up, he saw Virg Huckaby pushing into the center of the cleared area. As Kit Canfield righted himself, wheeled awkwardly, and started again for Shawn, the lawman caught him by the arms, pushed him back.

"Be enough of this!" the marshal snapped.

"Leave me be—damn you—" Canfield mumbled thickly. Wrenching free, he threw himself at Starbuck.

Shawn avoided the wildly swinging fists, maneuvered about to where he was behind the dazed rancher, and again taking him by the shoulders, propelled him toward one of the chairs and shoved him into it. Turning, Shawn motioned to Barney Canfield.

"He's your kin—look after him."

The younger brother's eyes flashed. "He's full growed —let him look after himself."

Continuing on, Starbuck returned to the table where Mason Lynch waited. He was breathing hard and several places in his body ached dully from the blows he'd taken from Kit Canfield. Picking up his mug of beer, he slaked the dryness in his throat, nodded crisply to Mason.

"Let's get out of here—get something to eat." His voice was taut, reflected the anger that still rolled through him.

Mason, smiling broadly, unable to hide his admiration, said, "Sure, sure—any time you're ready. Man, what a trimming you gave Kit! He'll be healing up from that one for a long time."

"Expect he'll live through—"

"What started this?"

At Huckaby's harshly put question, Shawn turned. He was expecting to be crawled by the lawman for becoming involved in the fight—but he was in no mood to take a tongue lashing for it.

55

"Kit—ordering us to ride out tonight," Lynch said, replying for Starbuck.

"I told you to stay out of trouble—"

"You should have told Canfield that!" Starbuck countered.

The lawman's lips pulled into a thin line and his small eyes sparked. Shifting his glance, he looked to where Kemmer's bartender was pouring a tumbler full of whiskey for the battered rancher. A subtle expression of satisfaction stole across Huckaby's features—and Shawn had a fleeting wonder as to his inner feelings—wondered, too, how long the marshal might have stood outside, beyond the swinging doors, and observed the fight before putting in his official appearance.

"Reckon Kit got more'n he bargained for," Huckaby said. "You're a real handy-andy with them fists of yours."

"His pa was a sort of champion," Mason volunteered. "Shawn learned from him."

A glass crashed to the floor, shattered, as Kit Canfield swept the table before him clean, struggled to his feet. Eyes blazing, he glared at the men surrounding him.

"Leave me alone! Don't need none of you—hear?"

His brother, Barney, the side of his face now swollen and discolored, moved in closer as the bystanders fell back. "Let's be getting back to the ranch, Kit. Supper'll be waiting, and we've got to—"

"The hell with the ranch—the hell with you!" the redhead shouted, stepping back. Colliding with a chair, he kicked it aside savagely. "The hell with every goddam one of you!" he added, and crossing to the doorway, knocked the batwings aside and disappeared into the street.

9

Silent and chagrined, Barney Canfield followed his brother into the falling darkness. Huckaby shook his head. "He ought to take Kit home. Be trouble around here tonight sure as hell, if he don't."

"Lock him up," Starbuck suggested indifferently.

The lawman brought his attention back to Shawn, squinted at him narrowly. "Just might do that, if it gets needful. Was a mighty fierce working-over you gave him. Did I hear Mason say you were some kind of a champion?"

"No, it was my pa—and he wasn't a champion, just plenty good at it."

"That buckle you're wearing, it yours or his?"

"His." Shawn glanced at Lynch. "We going after something to eat?"

Mason started to rise, hesitated as the marshal laid a hand on his shoulder, pressed him back.

"Was a man killed down in Las Cruces, over New Mexico way, about a year ago. Was by a fellow fighting the way you were doing—boxing as you call it."

Starbuck came to attention, not sure of what the lawman was getting at but instantly alerted, as always, when someone with training in scientific fisticuffs was mentioned; there was always the possibility that the person involved could be Ben.

"So?"

"Seeing you at it there set me to wondering—you ever in Las Cruces?"

Shawn laughed, the blunt accusation showing through the question. "Wasn't me, Marshal. Been through the town a couple of times but I never got in any fights. This man you're looking for, he charged with murder?"

"That's what it is—murder."

"How'd you hear about it?" Starbuck asked, sitting down and shoving a chair at Huckaby. "You get a wanted dodger on the man?"

Ordinarily such a poster would carry a picture of the sought-for criminal, or if none was available, a description would be given. Evidently the latter was true, otherwise Huckaby wouldn't have asked his question; but a detail of the boxer's appearance, and a name, could prove of great value in providing a lead on Ben.

"Nope, nothing like that," Huckaby said, settling onto the chair. "Sheriff of that county rode through asking about such a man. Asked me to keep my eyes peeled."

Shawn's hopes withered. "Well, sure wasn't me."

He let it drop there, not wishing to mention the name of Jim Ivory and the possibility of him being Ben. He was not certain if the lawman was acquainted with Ivory and he would as soon not point suspicion in that direction until he had met and talked with the man.

Huckaby said, "Didn't much think you were. Seems the fellow he was talking about was short, and he'd be older'n you, by several years, if I recollect rightly. You're sure going to need some helping going out to the Canfield's now. What time in the morning you want to leave?"

Shawn was only half listening, was already laying plans to visit the old settlement of The Crosses and make inquiries as to the boxer being sought for murder—should his meeting with Jim Ivory prove unproductive. It was not a comforting thought that Ben could be wanted by the law, but there was that possibility, since skilled boxers were not plentiful along the frontier.

"You hear me?"

Shawn became aware of the lawman's raised voice, said: "Sorry, Marshal, guess I was thinking hard. You ask me something?"

"Want to know what time we're riding out to the Box C."

"Any time suits me. How about nine o'clock? Feel like I'm going to be real lazy once I crawl into a bed."

"All right, nine o'clock," Huckaby said, and got to his feet. "Be seeing you then——"

"Marshal," Lynch broke in, "something I'd like to ask before you go."

Huckaby frowned, rested both hands on the back of his chair. "Let's hear it."

"The Hope family—they had that little place down by the creek—they still around?"

A stillness came into the lawman's features. "No, they moved away a long time back—leastwise, Tom and his missus did."

"The girl—Marie. What became of her?"

The lawman shrugged. "Reckon I'd forgot about Marie and you." He studied the backs of his weathered hands. "She's one of the women at Frisco's—bawdy house at the edge of town."

Mason's eyes closed slightly as if he had been struck with sudden and intense pain. He lowered his head. "How —what happened?"

"Same thing that usually happens to a lone woman. Her folks were around here for six, seven year after you left. Marie lived with them, had herself a job table-waiting at the old Elite Café, and then later on at Ma Chuckson's. Then she up and got herself married, and right after that her folks pulled out. Went back to Nebraska, somebody said."

"Who'd she marry?" Lynch asked with no great interest.

"Don't recollect his name now—didn't know him, actually. Was a cowhand working on a ranch east of here. Decent sort of fellow, I reckon, but he went and got himself killed—gored by a steer. Well, they didn't have no money, of course, so Marie came back here after it was all over, got herself a job in Newt Duckworth's saloon. Was all she could find.

"Then she up and quit there, sort of, well—dropped out of sight for a time. Next thing I knew she was at the Frisco House—and I didn't know that until she come in one day to bail out some drummer she'd been laying up with."

"God—I never thought . . ."

"Don't you go faulting her none!" Huckaby said sharply. "Was what she had to do, I reckon."

"Not blaming her," Lynch replied in a lifeless tone.

"Well, you want to see her, she'll be at the Frisco House. You know where it is."

"I know," Mason said.

The lawman nodded his head at Starbuck, turned away, and moved for the swinging doors. Shawn studied his friend's dark, bitter features for a long minute, and then realizing the man's trend of thought should best be changed, pushed back his chair.

"We were heading for a square meal," he said, "one that won't have a cupful of sand mixed in it. You know where this Ma Chuckson place is?"

Lynch stirred, got to his feet. "Next to the hotel."

Starbuck said, "Lead the way," and throwing a glance at the men still in the saloon, trailed Mason to the batwings and out onto the gallery that fronted the building. Again he looked over the room; no one had made a move to follow. He sighed gratefully, guessed the affray with Kit Canfield had generated no other challengers honing to try their skill, as was quite often the case; he was dog-tired and he had enough aches and bruises to last for a while.

"There it is," Lynch said, pointing to a low-roofed structure squatting alongside the Mogollon Hotel.

They crossed over, entered a clean, well-lit room where a dozen or so small tables with complementing quartettes of hard-backed chairs were distributed in a precise arrangement that made the most of all available space. Three were occupied, and Shawn and Mason selected a vacant one near the window. The street was quiet now as darkness had settled over the town, dispelling some of the heat and bringing a softness to the hardlined structures along the dusty way.

An elderly woman appeared, gave them an impersonal appraisal, took their orders for steak, potatoes, biscuits, and coffee without unnecessary comment, then returned to the rear of the establishment where the kitchen evidently lay, walking with the heavy-footedness of one sick to death of her work.

The meal was excellent in Starbuck's estimation, and Mason, now more silent and withdrawn than ever, laconically agreed. Finished, they went back to the street, stood for a time in the cool shadows, enjoying the break in the heat as the settlement gradually awoke to the night. But the day had been a long, hard one, and Starbuck began to consider the comforts of a soft bed. He glanced at the hotel.

"I'm about to get myself caught up with, so I think I'll turn in. You ready?"

Mason was staring off down the street toward a small, white church where a bell was tolling the members to evening prayer meeting.

"No—you go ahead. I'm kind of jumpy. Don't think I could go to sleep was I to try."

"You got something special in mind to do?"

Mason shook his head. "Thought maybe I'd mosey around a bit, just looking. Might visit Ma and Pa's graves, do a little listening to the church services."

"Go ahead. I'll get a room for the both of us. The clerk'll tell you which one."

60

"Fine," Lynch said and moved off into the soft darkness. "See you later."

Starbuck turned to the steps leading up onto the Mogollon's porch. "Good night," he answered.

10

Mason Lynch slowed, watched Shawn cross the hotel's narrow gallery and disappear through the doorway into the lobby. He moved on then, the irony of the situation striking hard at him in that moment; he was in his own home town, among persons he knew, perhaps had even grown up with, yet his only friend was an outsider—a stranger he had encountered on the trail.

But he guessed no one was to blame but himself, even for the way things had turned out for Marie Hope. If he hadn't lost his head that day and cut down Wade Canfield, like as not he and Marie would be happily raising a family and building a ranch—in that order—down in the Mescal Mountain country.

He strolled on, noting idly the storefronts—some familiar, some new: Dr. Amos Hewlett . . . Cornman's Hardware Store . . . Mrs. Broadwell, Ladies & Childrens Ready-to-Wear . . . Pete Gabaldon, Feed & Seed . . . Sam Lingle, Gen'l. Mdse. . . . His wandering gaze stopped on that long, narrow building with its warped, paint-scaled false front. Did Sam Lingle still own what evidently was still Lynchburg's largest store? Sam had been an old man fourteen years ago.

Traffic along the street was light, and he saw only a few persons along the plank sidewalks—none he recognized or that acknowledged him. Several men lounged around the front of the Maricopa, and as he passed, aware of the tinkling of the piano, the muffled drone of voices and smells of beer and whiskey, something was said and there was a cautious laugh among the loafers.

Mason dismissed it without second thought. In the decade that had passed under the most trying and degrading of circumstances, he had learned the futility of taking offense at every disparaging remark cast his way as well as acquiring a philosophy for survival—accept the cards dealt you, play them as best you can. There was actually little in life worth fighting for.

He drew abreast the Rawhide Saloon—Newt Duckworth's place—and slackened his step. Marie had been forced to work there for a time, he recalled Huckaby saying, and for several minutes he stood quietly in the warm night staring past the open doorway into the murky, smoke-filled depths of the small building.

It was hard to think of her working there—a third-rate establishment with no tables, no music, no gambling or dancing. What use would Duckworth have for a girl employee? His was the sort of place that catered to men seeking to get thoroughly and quietly drunk at the cheapest rates.

A yellow-wheeled surrey rolled into the north end of the street, its iron tires making a grating sound as they sliced through the sandy soil, the sleek-looking matched grays stepping proudly on their way to some destination at the opposite end of the settlement. A man and a woman occupied the front seat—two small children were in the rear. Strangers, too—newcomers to the area. Mason reconsidered that thought, corrected himself; after ten years' absence he reckoned he was the newcomer.

The strains of "Onward Christian Soldiers," sung with fervor and abetted by the solid thump of a piano, drifted to him from the open doorway of the church, now just ahead. With the hymn ringing in his ears, he entered the yard, circled the narrow, white structure with its steep, gable roof, came to the small cemetery lying behind it.

Weeds had made good progress with the two graves, and he spent a quarter-hour policing the mounds and resetting the wooden markers which time and the elements had conspired to tilt. The lettering, skillfully carved into the pine by the church sexton, was still legible, but just barely. Now that he had returned maybe he could replace the wood with stone or marble. It would take a little money, something he was plenty shy of at the moment, but later, perhaps—if things went well.

His thoughts halted as his eyes reached down the darkened street, moving past the squat adobe huts occupied by the Mexican people, and settled on the two-storied bulk of the Frisco House, standing silent and apart from all others.

Instantly Marie Hope was again in his mind, provoking memory, and giving rise to a vague, lonely aching. He was remembering her as he last saw her—dark eyes, smooth

63

face sober, hair gathered in a bun on her neck as she stood in the crowd and watched him, cuffed and shackled, climb into the stagecoach with the U.S. Marshal who was taking him to prison.

He never saw or heard from her after that final moment. No letter writer himself, he would have found little opportunity in those first two years behind the grim walls of the penitentiary, even had he been so inclined, as brutal punishment details, designed to break the will and spirit, were a daily fare.

And after that, when matters eased off more or less into a dreary, monotonous routine, it was too late. Marie would certainly have forgotten him, for no word had ever arrived from her—not that such was proof she had never written; letters from home, more often than prison officials would admit, somehow failed to get delivered. But it was better to assume that she had forgotten him, had simply given him up; it was the only practical thing for her to do.

Now he wondered about her; had she changed? Would she be thinking of him, too, when word of his return reached the Frisco House—which it probably had by that hour? He shrugged. Likely Marie would give him no thought at all. He was a closed chapter in her life—meant nothing. Unquestionably the years of bitter tribulations had marked her appearance; as to her heart and soul, there could be no doubt of it.

Crossing to a log bench someone had thoughtfully placed beneath the spreading trees at the edge of the fenced plot, Mason sat down. The lilacs strung along the back of the area had bloomed and were now without fragrance; but wafting in from some close-by location was the odor of honeysuckle, and he sat for a time enjoying its sweetness and remembering how his mother had coddled and coaxed a vine to grow above the kitchen window of the old place.

The singing inside the church had ended and he could hear the deep-throated voice of a man—the minister, he assumed—exhorting his flock to walk the path of righteousness. The words were mostly unintelligible to Lynch but their urgency was undeniable, and he thought back to long ago when he, too, at the inflexible insistence of his parents, had regularly taken his place on one of the hard-bottomed pews and been fed a diet of salvation.

Those had been good times, and recalling them awakened pleasant memories; but there was no profit in thinking of days gone—for there was no method of changing what had happened. He had come to realize that just as no man had ever yet found a place where he could hide from himself, so also was it equally impossible for him to undo the mistakes he had made. It was a fact of life of which he had always been aware, but it had taken a decade for him to fully comprehend the meaning.

Head down, Mason sat in the darkness of the sweetly scented night, only partly conscious of the singing again pouring from the throat of the little church, of the black, star-spangled canopy above him, of the gradually decreasing activity along the street as the hour grew late. He knew only a nagging, persistent longing that throbbed deep in his mind to see Marie, perhaps even talk to her. What she was now did not matter, nor was there any desire within him to avail himself of her talents; it was senseless, useless, but the need simply to look at her once more was pushing at him with irresistible force.

Rising, he started back through the cemetery, following the path that wound among the graves and led finally to the churchyard. The congregation had departed, and glancing through the still-open doorway into the lighted sanctuary, he could see the minister, a tall, lonely figure, standing off to one side reading from a book.

Continuing, Mason turned into the narrow side street and made his way along the darkened huts toward the distant, taller structure of the Frisco House. Now and then a dog barked at his passage, and once he heard a child crying as if frightened by something in the dark.

Arriving there, he halted in the shadow of the long-abandoned stable that stood directly across from the large building. Once the place had been a stopping point for stagecoaches, with the depot on the ground floor, the upper level arranged in a series of rooms available to travelers who wished to lay over, rest briefly from whatever rigorous journey they were making. The stable where the teams were fed and sheltered had been erected conveniently near, with the holding corral—now a square of staggering, rotting posts—to the south.

All had been abandoned for newer quarters in the settlement at some time during the years when he was away fighting the war, and a minor boom was taking place in Lynchburg. It had been called the Frisco House then, and as is quite often the way, the name stuck, was never dropped regardless of the change in the nature of the tenantry.

It now appeared to be in total darkness, but it was a deceptive impression. Light streaks lay along the edge of shades not completely drawn or that ill fitted their window

65

frames, and from the squares of different-colored glass panes making up the front door—once a solid slab of thick wood—there issued a muted glow.

Abruptly that door opened and a slash of lamplight broke through the night, illuminating a rectangle of the weedy yard momentarily and offering a quick glimpse into the garishly furnished entry hall before it swung closed again.

The man who had emerged made his way unsteadily along the well-beaten walk, veering sharply once when his faltering legs carried him into a thorny bush of wild roses, came finally to the street. He pulled to a wavering halt there, got his bearings firmly established, and then began the trek back to the settlement.

Lynch stood for a time contemplating the weaving shadow, seemingly ricocheting from one side of the roadway to the other, and when it had at last vanished into the darkness, brought his eyes back to the building before him.

Uncertainty again possessed him. There was no sensible reason to see Marie, much less talk with her. It could result only in the reopening of old wounds, raking fresh the thinly healed scars. Yet . . .

On impulse he stepped from the doorway of the stable, crossed the street, and started up the path leading to the front steps. Reaching there he once more paused, torn again by indecision. He swore silently at himself; once such irresolution had been no part of his character—but after ten years during which all thinking, all decisions had been done for him, it had become a way of life.

Still vacillating, he turned from the path, moved to the window immediately to his left, where a strip of light separated the shade's lower edge and the sill. It would be better, perhaps, first to have a look inside. Standing close to the wall, he peered through the narrow opening. This had been the main room of the depot, he recalled. Now it was the Frisco House's parlor, replete with plush chairs and couches, a massive table with fancy, scrolled legs, carpeting on the floor and framed prints on the papered walls.

A thick-bodied woman was in one of the larger chairs. Her hair was a startling yellow, like the goldpoppys that cover the slopes in spring, and as she knitted at some sort of garment, face tipped down, she was talking steadily.

Mason shifted to the opposite side of the window, where he had a different view of the room. Two younger women were seated on a couch placed against the near wall, one leafing through an old, well-handled magazine, the other staring absently at one of the pictures on the wall. He felt his throat tighten as he recognized the latter. It was Marie.

In silence he stood there, leaning against the cool stone of the old building, eyes riveted to the girl. She had changed, of course. Thinner by considerable, her face almost gaunt and now turned ugly by the rouge and rice powder so generously applied. But her eyes were the same —or so he thought. A moment later she turned and looked directly toward the window as if suspecting someone's presence.

There was change. No longer did they have the soft, doelike quality that had made of her, a girl of only ordinary attractiveness, one of quiet, stirring beauty. Her eyes now were dull, sunken, filled with a listlessness that bespoke the desperation that filled her.

Mason Lynch drew back, a sickness gripping him. He had made her that way. He had been the cause of it—him and his anger and his unwillingness to accept what he did not want to face. Now it was too late to make amends, to try and right the wrong he had done. Or was it? Should he talk to her, tell her of his plans for the place in the Mescals—ask her to become a part of it, of his future? Would she listen—or would she laugh in his face?

The light running sound of an approaching horse reached him. He glanced to the street. A rider was coming up from town. Stepping into the tangle of unkempt shrubbery growing along the wall, he watched the horseman, vaguely familiar, swing into the stable, reappear shortly on foot. Entering the yard, he crossed to the porch in purposeful steps and halted before the door.

The night suddenly echoed with his impatient pounding as he demanded entry. The door flung back. Mason's lips curled as light fell upon the now easily recognizable figure of Kit Canfield. Then all was again plunged into darkness as the rancher entered and the multicolored panel closed behind him.

For several moments Mason Lynch did not stir, and then drawn by some irresistible force, he returned to his place at the window. Canfield, a bottle of whiskey in one hand, had entered the room, was standing before the two girls on the couch. His face was swollen, dark with bruises from the beating Shawn Starbuck had given him, and as he reached down, grasped Marie by the wrist, and pulled her upright, there was a brutish anticipation in the slackness of his hard grin.

Pushing her toward the stairway, he followed, saying something to the woman with the yellow hair as he passed, laughed. The woman joined in, dutifully it seemed, and thoughtfully watched the rancher climb the steps; then shaking her head, she resumed her knitting.

Mason continued to stand at the window, staring into the room but seeing nothing while an unreasoning, towering rage hammered at him. Kit Canfield and Marie—his Marie! Goddam the man to hell! If he had a gun he'd . . . he'd . . .

Town Marshal Virgil Huckaby stood in the dark passageway separating Spearman's and the widow Broadwell's establishments, and there wholly unnoticed by the few persons wandering along the street soaking in the evening coolness, maintained his watch on the side door of Duckworth's saloon, into which Kit Canfield had disappeared an hour or so earlier.

There was no mystery as to what lay behind the door; it was the living quarters of the new girl Duckworth had brought in from Prescott to work for him. By rights she should be in the saloon now, helping Newt behind the counter. He had discovered, more or less by accident, that such was good for business—a well-rounded, skimpily clad female bartender—but Kit, in his usual loud and despotic manner, had claimed her services and Duckworth was being forced to cope with customers alone. Kit, however, would have his fill of her shortly, permitting her to return to regular duties—and thus turn Canfield loose on the town again.

For this Virg Huckaby waited hopefully. Not that the rancher's insatiable hunger for women, so strong as to often require the services of several during a single night, was of particular interest to the lawman; likely, fired with liquor, goaded into a searing fury by the licking he had so publicly taken in the Maricopa, it was only logical to expect this would be just such a night—and God pity the whores he bedded down! The man was a sadist at heart and he'd be taking out his rage and frustration on each of them.

All of which was nothing new to Huckaby; he'd seen Canfield in similar moods before, had on occasion seen fit to step in, cover for the man's actions, all in the interests of the town—but that was over now. Kit had drawn a sharp and definite line, making it clear where he stood and what his intentions were. Now, as far as Virgil Huckaby was concerned, all the bars were down and Kit Canfield had best look to his hindquarters—for one slip on his part and the wolves would close in.

Lock him up! Starbuck had said earlier that evening when he had mentioned the possibility of trouble from Kit after he had gone storming out of the Maricopa. *Lock him up!* Why not? If he could nail Canfield for doing something that was a clear violation of the law—why not? He could expect no mercy from the rancher—why not simply beat him to the punch?

He guessed he hadn't ever really understood how deep his hatred for the swaggering, loud-mouthed rancher was until that afternoon late when Kit had voiced his threats. Of course there had never been any cordiality between them, the lawman having categorized and pegged Kit Canfield for what he was the first day they met. And then when the Mason Lynch murder thing had been settled and much later, after Marie Hope had married, lived for a time with a husband, and become widowed, the feeling toward the rancher had intensified even more.

Virg had thought a lot about Marie, had not only felt sorry for her because of the turn fate had given her, but had known a genuine affection, entertaining thoughts of asking her to marry him despite the fact he was old enough to be her father. And it seemed to him he was making progress along such lines, too.

Then Kit Canfield became aware of Marie's obvious charms—a young widow in the full bloom of early womanhood—and moved in. In a short time he had completely overcome her, swung her to his way of thinking, and if she had ever seriously considered wedding the lawman, it was blasted to the winds by the rancher's swashbuckling, free-spending manner.

He'd had some rough moments there in the Maricopa when Mason Lynch had asked about Marie, and what he had been forced to say had ripped open all of the old sores, set them to festering again. He owed Kit Canfield plenty, not only for Marie, who, tired of within a few months by the rancher who kept her in lonely splendor and solitude in a cottage at the edge of town, eventually ended up in the Frisco House, but for all the insults, the humiliation, and the sly, steady undermining of his position in the town as well. . . .

His morose thinking came to a halt, as down the street he saw Mason Lynch emerge from the churchyard, where he had evidently been visiting his folks' graves. Mason paused, then moved off through Mexicantown—on his way, no doubt, to pay a call on Marie Hope.

Mason was a fool to do that, he thought. He would find nothing but disappointment and disillusionment; things can never be put back in proper order once a change has been made. Physically, perhaps; in all other ways, no. Mason Lynch would be better off to turn around, come back— forget about the girl he had once planned to make his wife.

He watched Lynch's slight figure dissolve into the shadows, listened idly to the dogs tracing the man's passage with their successive barks, brought his eyes back to Duckworth's. Homer Boyd, in company with Doc Hewlett, strolled along the street on the opposite side, bearing for a final nightcap at the Maricopa.

If he could manage to get something on Kit Canfield, could he expect Boyd and the rest of the merchants to stand by him? Or would they think only of their pocketbooks and back the rancher?

He didn't like the answer that came so readily to mind; a marshal would be easy to replace—a successful rancher pouring thousands of dollars into a town's business firms each year would not. It would take something really serious to turn people from Kit. Fighting, drunkenness—such simple infractions as that were out; it would require a coldblooded killing, or the rape of a decent woman—preferably a young girl—to bring him down. And while he was capable of both he was much too clever to get caught at it.

But he had to find an answer. Canfield had thrown his cards face up on the table, made it plain what he intended to do; Huckaby had accepted the challenge, declared it a fight to the finish. He was only sorry that Kit's encounter with Starbuck had ended as it had, wished instead, with no qualms, that it had gone a step farther, and the rancher, completely losing his head, had reached for his pistol. Starbuck, who undoubtedly was a gunman, would have shot him dead. That would have settled things once and for all.

He drew to quiet attention as Duckworth's side door opened. The girl appeared, circled to the front of the saloon, and entered. She was back shortly, carrying a quart bottle of whiskey, and re-entered her quarters. She did not remain, however, simply left the liquor with Kit, and retracing her steps to the saloon, took her place behind the bar.

Kit evidently liked what he found in the girl, planned to spend the remainder of the night with her. She would probably be going off duty in another hour or two. Huckaby, disappointed, rubbed at his jaw, shrugged. He might as well give it up until morning. Maybe it would be smart to get with Duckworth's new girl, see if something could be set up.

The door opened again. Canfield, bottle clutched in his hand, stepped out into the shadows lying alongside the saloon. He stalled for the space of time required to take a drink of the liquor, and then wheeling, circled back behind the building to the rack where his horse waited.

Shortly he was again in view, slumped in the saddle, the black he was riding moving at a tired walk as he turned into the street and headed south—for the Frisco House.

Virg Huckaby delayed until the rancher had been swallowed by the darkness beyond the church, and then, careful not to be seen by any of the few persons remaining abroad, he doubled back to the alley, and followed.

11

Starbuck sat up, roused from a sound slumber by a pounding on his door. Reaching instinctively for the pistol hanging in its belt from the back of a nearby chair, he glanced to his left. That side of the bed was empty. Mason Lynch had not returned.

Frowning, he threw his legs over the edge, drew on his britches, and moved to the door, wondering, dully, if the hotel clerk had forgotten to give Mason the key left at the desk for him, wondering, also, what time of the night it was; somewhere around two or three o'clock, he guessed.

The insistent hammering came again. Shawn, now fully awake and cautious, stepped to the left of the panel.

"Who's there?"

"Huckaby." The lawman's answer was quick, blunt. "Open up, Starbuck!"

Shawn thrust his forty-five under the waistband of his pants, picked up the extra key he had obtained, and turned the lock. In the dim glow of the hallway's bracketed lamp, he saw the marshal, Fred Kemmer, and three or four other men. Their faces were grim.

"What's the trouble?" he asked, but a deep worry was beginning to move through him; this had something to do with Mason. Turning, he halted beside the table, struck a match to the lamp's wick, and as the yellow glow spread over the room, came about. He saw then that Huckaby had his pistol in his hand, ready.

"Where's Lynch?" the lawman demanded, eyes prowling the room.

Starbuck shook his head. "Not here yet. Wasn't ready for sleeping when I was. Left him standing out there on the street."

Kemmer, his fleshy face sallow in the weak light, nodded to the marshal. "That proves it. It was him that did it."

"Did what?" Starbuck asked patiently. "Let's have it, Huckaby—what's this all about?"

The lawman leaned against the washstand, folded his arms across his chest. "You certain you don't know?"

"How the hell would I know anything? Been in this bed since first part of the evening."

"You prove that?"

"Say!" Kemmer exclaimed, a brightness coming into his eyes. "You maybe've got something there, Virg! Why couldn't it've been him? He had trouble with Kit in my place. Could have hunted him up, finished him off."

Huckaby, head cocked to one side, impassively studied Shawn. "You got an answer for that?"

Shawn stirred indifferently. "Might—if I knew what you're getting at." His hunch had been right, apparently. Something had occurred and they were suspecting Mason —even him—of doing it.

The lawman continued to stare for a long breath and then said, "Kit Canfield got killed tonight. Murdered."

Starbuck came up slowly, but it was no big surprise; men such as Canfield never live to a ripe age. In that next moment the full implication of the lawman's words and presence came to him.

"And you think Mason Lynch did it?"

"Or maybe you," Kemmer said slyly.

Shawn favored the saloonman with a withering look, "You're a damned fool, mister." He put his attention on Huckaby. "You're wrong, Marshal, if that's what you're thinking. Mason wouldn't have done it—I'm sure of that."

"Why not? He still hated the Canfields—still packed that big grudge."

"And Kit was killed with his own gun," one of the other men said. "Means the man who shot him didn't have no iron of his own. Virg has got Lynch's over to his office."

"That proves nothing," Starbuck said, drawing on the remainder of his clothing, "except that Canfield knew whoever it was, figured him for a friend and let him get up close. Where'd it happen?"

"Out in front of the Frisco House," Huckaby said. "Seems Kit was there late—stayed on quite a spell. Mason must've been there, too, waiting in the old stable across the road."

The Frisco House . . . the girl named Marie Hope . . . Shawn was thinking back, remembering what had been said about her. Once she had meant a great deal to Mason

73

—it was possible she still did; in fact, he himself had suggested Mason should see her. And Virg Huckaby was aware of the connection, too, would be remembering.

"Anybody see Mason around there?" he asked casually.

Huckaby nodded slowly. "One of the women seen a man standing in the dark inside the stable. Claims she didn't know him but she'd recognize him again, was she to see him."

"Standing in the dark?"

"Expect there was a little light."

Starbuck finished his dressing. "Somebody—but not exactly Mason Lynch. Way you're all putting it, sounds like you're sure it was him."

"Mighty hard to believe it wasn't," Kemmer said. "I'll lay you odds that Lynch came back here with that in his mind all the time—to square up with the Canfields like he started out to do ten years ago."

Shawn strapped on his pistol. "That's a bet I'd win. Mason's had enough punishment. He's not going to let something he no longer cares a whit about get him in trouble again." Glancing up to Huckaby, he added, "What about me? Decided whether I'm guilty or not?"

The lawman shrugged. "I'll tell you this—you ain't out of the woods yet."

"Well, if there's any doubt, you might ask the clerk downstairs. He'll tell you I never left the place after I turned in. Knew I'd be sleeping hard so I left the extra key for Mason at the desk."

"Which he never come back and used," Kemmer said pointedly. "Means he's skipped out."

"Not for sure," Starbuck replied, stubbornly.

"Then where the hell is he?" Huckaby shouted, suddenly angered. "He ain't here and we've looked all over town."

"What about his horse? It gone?"

"Going there next," the marshal said after a long breath during which he and Kemmer exchanged glances. Evidently they had overlooked that possibility, were trying now to make it appear no oversight. "Figured to come here first."

Starbuck grunted, pulled on the old hat he still had not found time to replace, and turned to the door. It was a bit strange that the lawman had searched the town for Mason Lynch before coming to the most logical place to seek him —in his hotel room. And the part about his horse; that, too, would seem to be one of the things that would be checked on at the very beginning.

"You seem plenty sure it was Mason," he said again. "Looks like you could've done more about it than just hunt for him."

"He's the one with the reason—"

"You telling me Kit Canfield didn't have any enemies?" Shawn asked, eyeing the lawman narrowly as they moved down the hall and began to descend the stairs. "I got the idea he was a man with more'n his share. Pretty plain you're included in that bunch, too."

Huckaby's expression did not alter. "Ain't denying it. Never did like Kit. Always throwing his weight around. But I managed to get along with him."

"Hell," Kemmer said deprecatingly, "like to see the man who doesn't have a few enemies. But Kit's weren't the murdering kind, just soreheads."

"Any man with a grudge can turn into the murdering kind," Starbuck said as they started across the lobby.

"And you're claiming Mason Lynch wasn't carrying one?"

"I am. Whole thing was a lost cause far as he was concerned. Same as told me he wouldn't have his folk's old place back as a gift."

Kemmer laughed. "And you believed that?"

"Yes," Shawn said quietly as they stepped out onto the porch of the Mogollon, "I believed him." He pulled up short, anger and disgust stirring through him. Several men had gathered in the street, were waiting in the cool darkness. One, a coiled rope hooked over his left shoulder, was fashioning a hangman's noose. Abruptly he wheeled to Huckaby.

"What kind of law is this?"

The marshal shook his head. "Not my idea. These men have got their minds pretty well made up." Moving to the edge of the gallery, he motioned to the man with the rope. "Put that away, Harry. Ain't going to be no lynching around here."

Harry did not cease his methodic shaping of the knot. "Nothing wrong with being ready."

Starbuck spat, dropped off the porch, and turned toward Fortney's livery stable. No lights burned along the silent street, not even in the saloons, and the only sounds to be heard were those made by the men trooping along through the dust. Huckaby forged up to a position ahead of Shawn.

"Never mind," he said drily, "I'll take charge."

"Then do it!" Starbuck snapped. "We find Mason at the

75

stable, that bunch of vigilantes back there had better keep calm or I'll use my gun!"

"You'll do what I tell you—same as they will," Huckaby said stiffly. "Thing I'm looking out for here is that you don't get in the way, let him make a run for it if he's holed up."

"If I knew where he was, I sure wouldn't be leading you and that crowd to him—"

"Didn't figure you would, but was we to bump into him accidental-like, could be you'd try making it easy for him."

Shawn made no reply not certain in his own mind how he would react if they did encounter Lynch. He felt sure the man was not guilty of Kit Canfield's death, yet he could not forget Mason had practiced deceit on him after they had met. Even so, if it did develop that Lynch was guilty, he'd still be unable simply to draw back, see him pay for the crime at the hands of a hanging party.

Ahead of him the lawman halted. The wide, double doors of Fortney's were open, as was customary on summer nights, but the lantern ordinarily hanging in the runway was missing.

Huckaby drew his pistol, glanced at Shawn. "Pretty sure he's hiding in there. You want to try some talking, see if you can get him to give up without a fuss?"

Starbuck stepped into the opening. "Mason!" he called. "It's Shawn. You in there?"

A muffled answer of some sort came from the tack room on the left. Instantly Huckaby whirled and hurried to it, the men behind him following quickly. Starbuck, off to one side, drew his pistol, waited. A match flared in the gloom, and shortly a lantern's glow spread through the area.

"It's Ernie!" a voice shouted. "He's been tied up!"

Starbuck slid his weapon back into its holster; he had been certain it would be someone other than Mason Lynch, but he was taking no chance. Jaw set, he crossed the runway, shouldered his way through the men crowded around the door that led into the small anteroom. For the first time since Virg Huckaby and the others had appeared in his hotel quarters, he was having doubts. The answer would lie with the hostler; he wanted to hear it first hand.

Huckaby was slicing through the light rope that bound the elderly man's wrists, Kemmer was tugging at the gag. It came loose and the oldster hawked, spat angrily.

"Consarned stinking rag—"

"Who was it, Ernie?" Huckaby asked, closing his knife as the cotton strands parted. "You get a look at him?"

"Look—hell, I was talking to him!"

"Was it Mason Lynch?"

"That's who it was—Mason Lynch! Come bustin' in here all in a hurry for his horse. Tried to tell him that nag of his'n wasn't in no shape to travel, but he wouldn't listen. Saddled up and *then*, before he left, tied me good. Took my gun, too."

Huckaby, a smugness spread across his features, glanced at Starbuck, turned back to the hostler.

"How long ago was this?"

"Couple—no, I reckon it was about three hours."

Shawn felt Kemmer's eyes upon him, heard the man say: "Reckon that ought to prove who did it. You satisfied?"

"Only proves that he's gone—not that he did it," Starbuck said. He realized he sounded thick-skulled and arbitrary but it was difficult to believe that Mason Lynch could have undergone so drastic a change in mind and outlook.

He swung to Huckaby. "Marshal, have you stopped to think that Mason might've heard about the killing, and knowing he'd be blamed first off, got scared and left town fast as he could? He hasn't forgot that you had to keep a lynch mob off him ten years ago."

"No, I reckon I haven't," the lawman drawled, "but I expect, was I to set my mind to it, I could come up with a whole bunch of fancy tales like that."

"Could have been the way of it," Shawn insisted, hanging on to his temper.

"If so, then he'd a been smart to come right to me, not make things worse by hightailing it out of town."

"Time like that it's not easy for a man to think straight."

"Can't see as it bales hay one way or another what we think," Kemmer said. "Point is he's gone—and while we're standing here jawing, he's putting miles between us."

"That's right," one of the men in the crowd said. "Let's get mounted up and a-going after him."

"You see in the dark, Ike?" Huckaby asked in a mild voice. "That's what it'll take." He came about to where the hostler was now sitting, chafing his ankles ruefully. "You got any idea what direction he rode off in, Ernie?"

"Nope. Throwed back there in the corner like I was, I couldn't see nothing."

Huckaby rubbed at his chin. "Well, he won't be travel-

77

ing fast. We can start tracking him soon's it's daylight." He glanced toward the street. A half-dozen riders were wheeling in from the west, slowing, and then pounding on for the stable when they caught sight of the gathering.

"It's Barney," the rider called Harry, still fiddling with his rope, said. "Got some of the Box C boys with him. Somebody must've sent word to him."

"I did," the lawman said. "Right after Kit was found."

"He won't be much for waiting around for morning," Kemmer said. "He'll decide quick it was Lynch who done it when he hears he's lit out. He'll want to do something about it right now."

"You figure he can see in the dark like Ike?" Huckaby demanded sarcastically. "We'll go after him, but there ain't no use starting—"

"You got him?" Barney Canfield's hard voice shouted from the runway.

"Who?" the marshal asked.

"Lynch—who the hell you think? Was him that did it, wasn't it?"

"Way it looks," Ike said before Huckaby could speak. "He's long gone."

The rancher strode angrily into the crowd of men. "Gone?"

"Sure is. Come and got his horse and run for it. Tied up Ernie so's he couldn't set up a holler."

"Then let's get a posse mounted and start beating the brush," Canfield snapped. "Sooner we get after him, sooner we can nail him down."

"Posse won't be necessary," Starbuck said, raising his voice above the hubbub. Moving through the gathering, he halted in front of Huckaby. "Marshal, I want you to deputize me. I'll go after Mason by myself. Like to see him brought in alive."

The silence following Starbuck's words was long and complete. Barney Canfield broke it. "The hell you will!"

A welter of words broke out, some angry, all frankly skeptical. Shawn waited until the racket had died off.

"I'll tell you this, Marshal," he said, "you let this mob find him and you'll have a dead man on your hands—an innocent dead man."

The rancher spat. "Your job was to keep an eye on Lynch. If you'd've done the job, we wouldn't be here now."

"Not exactly the way I understood it," Shawn replied.

"Was the way I meant it!" Huckaby snapped.

Starbuck shrugged. He guessed he should have taken the lawman's words more seriously; he doubted, however, if it would have made any difference. Likely Mason Lynch would have done what he pleased. But perhaps the thought could be turned to his advantage.

"Good reason why it ought to be me that runs him down," he said.

A slyness came into Virgil Huckaby's eyes. "Maybe so. You got some idea where he'll go?"

"Nothing for sure. He mentioned a few things that might help."

"Like what?" Barney Canfield asked quickly.

Starbuck gave the rancher a dry smile. "I'm not about to tell you—or anybody else—not the way things are around here."

"I'm the law," Huckaby said. "You'll tell me, or I'm slapping you in jail."

Shawn hadn't considered that possibility. Now he studied the marshal narrowly. Huckaby was bluffing, he concluded.

"Suit yourself," he said. "I figure I can find him, but it'll

79

have to be on my terms. You don't go for that, then forget it."

"Just what we're going to do," Canfield stated, loud and flat. "Like as not the two of you are working together, anyway. Maybe you'd find him, but it'd be to join up so's the both of you could keep riding. Boys, I'm calling for a posse. Everyone of you willing to—"

"Back up, now, Barney," Huckaby cut in, stepping into the center of the room. "Posse comes under the heading of my business, and it'll take its orders from me."

The rancher bobbed his head, smiled. " 'Scuse me, Virg. I know that, but I want to get things started. I don't aim to let my brother's killer get away. Want to say right now, I'll pay a hundred dollars gold to the man who gets him."

"Dead or alive?" a voice asked.

"Makes no difference to me—"

"It damn well does to me!" Huckaby said, raising his hands for silence. "Any of you aiming to ride along is going to take my orders. That don't suit your fancy, then pull out now, go home, don't mix in. That clear?"

There was no direct reply, only a murmur and a shuffling of booted feet on the dusty floor.

"All right, then," the lawman continued. "Let's get this thing organized. Couple of you trot over to Yaqui Joe's, roust him out. Bring him to Kemmer's place. We'll start from there soon's it's light."

"What do we have to wait for?" Canfield protested. "Why ain't we leaving now?"

"Nobody knows what direction he took off in," Kemmer explained.

"Would've rode south—for the border," Canfield said. "That'd be my guess."

Shawn felt a twinge of alarm. In his judgment also, Mason would have taken that route, not for the border however, but for the Mescals, where he could hide out and rest the bay until the horse was better able to travel. Fortunately, no one in the crowd seemed to remember Lynch's place.

"New Mexico line's closer," a hooknosed puncher commented. "Was it me, I'd take my chances that way. 'Specially was I forking a lame horse."

"Yeh, reckon you could be right," the rancher said. He sucked at his lips, glanced over the crowd. "Virg's right. It'll be smart to wait for daylight, then put the Indian on his trail. Meanwhile, we can do our congregating at Kemmer's, sort of get set."

"Want everybody on a fresh horse," Huckaby said. "Ain't no telling how far we'll be riding."

"Till we catch him, that's how far," Canfield said. "Want that understood. Nobody quits and goes home till we've got him caught—and took care of." He paused, looked around, and then pointed at Starbuck. "What about him?"

"He's coming with us," the lawman said promptly. "Claims he's got some idea of where Mason might've gone. Fine. I figure if the trail Yaqui Joe digs up heads off in the direction Starbuck's thinking of—then we can make a straight run for whatever it is he's got in mind, save ourselves a lot of time that'd be lost in tracking."

Canfield nodded slowly. "Sounds good but maybe you're overlooking one thing—how do you know he'll tell us?"

Huckaby smiled grimly. "Oh, he'll talk up, all right. Don't worry about it."

Shawn looked closely at the lawman, also smiled. "That mean I'm being arrested?"

"More or less," the marshal replied. "Main thing, I want you handy so's we can find Lynch, get this thing squared away. Play it smart and everything'll work out fine for you." Huckaby hesitated, eyes on the men clustered around Barney Canfield and shifting toward the doorway. "Now, you get your horse, meet us at the saloon."

Starbuck watched the marshal turn away, become a part of the general exodus. Riding with Huckaby and his posse was the last thing he had in mind to do; what must be done was find Mason Lynch, warn him, and get him safely to some other town until the matter of Kit Canfield's death could be straightened out.

It could be possible that Mason, in a fit of anger, had killed the rancher, although Shawn still found the idea hard to accept. But if it did turn out to be a fact, then Lynch was entitled to a trial before a judge and jury and not deserving of rope justice—which was what he would get if the posse caught up with him. Perhaps Virg Huckaby sincerely believed he could control Canfield and those who would be riding with him, but there was every doubt in Starbuck's mind.

The last of the men had gone. Wheeling, Shawn stepped out into the runway. It was best he act quickly, gain all the time he could. Moving along the row of stalls until he came to the one in which the sorrel stood, he entered, began to throw his gear into place. Finished, he took the gelding's headstall in his hand, backed him into the run-way.

Allowing the reins to trail on the littered floor, Starbuck turned, trotted to the yet open double doors, peered into the street. Lights were now on in the Maricopa and a few horses were tied at the hitchrack; the posse was beginning to assemble. He probed the surrounding area carefully. No one was in sight.

But it would be smart to take no chances—use the sta-ble's rear entrance; in so doing he could be certain that his riding off alone rather than joining with the others form-ing the posse at the Maricopa—as he had been ordered by Huckaby to do—would not be noticed. Returning to the sorrel, he took up the reins and moved into the gloom fill-ing the rear of the barn.

13

☆

Starbuck reached the end of the runway, cut right into an aisle angling in from that point. The rear door was directly ahead. He halted. It was too easy. It didn't seem likely that Marshal Virg Huckaby would put him under arrest, more or less, order him to report later at the place where the posse was to assemble—and then simply walk away and let him do as he wished.

He considered that improbability for a full minute, and then deciding that, if so, two could play at the game of cleverness, and moved on, stopping again a half stride in the open. Poised there, he cocked his ear into the night. There was only the calm silence of the early hour. Still leading the sorrel, he stepped farther into the clear, away from the barn, paused. The hush persisted and his searching glance found nothing suspicious. He guessed he had misjudged the lawman; there appeared to be no one watching the livery stable after all.

Turning, he swung onto the saddle, kneed the gelding gently, sent him walking briskly down the lane between the wagon yard and a corral. Fortunately he was moving away from the buildings and the town itself, thus would run no risk of being spotted from the street. All he need do was proceed on a direct line and he would soon be in the low, brush-covered hills to the west of the settlement. Once there he would be free to move as he wished without fear of being observed.

Cigarette smoke . . .

At the first pungent whiff borne to him in the slight breeze, Starbuck drew up short. He'd been right. Huckaby was keeping an eye on him—undoubtedly had a man watching the front of Fortney's, too. He smiled grimly into the darkness. Huckaby was not about to let him slip off and find Mason Lynch on his own; he was permitting

83

him to go but he and the posse would be following at a discreet distance.

Silent, Shawn hunched over the saddle, pulled his feet free of the stirrups, and dropped to the ground, thus eliminating the silhouette his sitting high on the gelding afforded. Standing in the cool semi-darkness behind the stable, he tried to locate the source of the tobacco smoke, reasoning that since it came in to him on the breeze, the man would be somewhere directly ahead—to the west.

Cautious, he started forward, halted as not one but a pair of small, red eyes glowing in the night appeared on his left. The eyes brightened and dulled with pulsing regularity. Huckaby had put two men on the job.

Shawn considered that. One could be to hurry with the word of his so-called escape to the lawman, waiting with the remainder of the posse at Kemmer's saloon; the second could have been directed to follow, leaving suitable trail markings and signs for them to go by.

Virg Huckaby had him, Shawn recognized the fact. The lay of the land was such that he was forced to pass directly in front of the men if he intended to reach the hills. Nor was there an alternative; he could expect the street side of Fortney's to be under surveillance, also. All he could do was play out the hand, endeavor to outsmart the lawman in some way.

Mounting, Starbuck again moved forward. Instantly the twin glows disappeared. They had seen him, had rid themselves of their smokes. Keeping his eyes straight ahead, Starbuck rode on.

Shortly he came to the first of the sand hills, turned into a narrow draw crowded with sage and other rank growth, pressed on, resisting the almost overpowering urge to look back, see if Huckaby's men were following the plan he had assumed.

A hundred yards later he swung left, and urging the gelding to an easy trot, continued due south until he was well below the town. There, once again he altered direction, aiming deliberately for the rugged, rock-studded butte area sprawling like a great, ugly scar east of the settlement.

Once inside the welter of boulders, overhanging ledges, and tall mesquite, he ventured his first glance to the rear —almost instantly located a lone pursuer. The man was following his trail patiently in the pale light of the stars. There was no sign of a second tracker; it evidently had been as he suspected, and likely at that very moment Huckaby and his posse were preparing to get underway.

The country turned rougher, grew steadily wilder. On all sides now were ragged-faced buttes, arroyos that were deep-cut and twisting, filled with mesquite, greasewood, and hedges of tough Apache plume. It was all somewhat of a surprise to Shawn Starbuck; he did not expect to see so much desert growth this far in. It was as if a section of that harsh, burning country miles to the south and west had been lifted bodily by some gigantic hand and arbitrarily set down in an area given over primarily to forested, grassy hills.

He should be changing course again, not get too deep into the brake before he put into effect his plan for finding Mason Lynch. But the maneuver would require skill; he must be certain the rider dogging his tracks did not suspect. He glanced about, eyes straining in the half-light to see clearly his surroundings. He was presently following a fairly well-defined path that wound in and out of the rocks and brush as it gradually ascended to a mesa, dimly visible farther on.

Abruptly the path veered into a narrow aisle lying between almost perpendicular walls of reddish earth. Shawn halted, eyes on the ground. Hoofprints were plentiful in the space between the formations, indicating that the passage was undoubtedly the sole route for reaching the plateau on beyond the brake.

He rode the sorrel into the passageway for a short distance, then backed him out. Once again in the wider area he swung the gelding off into the thick brush, and there, well concealed, waited. Within few minutes Huckaby's man came into view, a hunched shape on his saddle, patiently working out the path.

Shawn delayed until he was certain the rider had entered the narrow pass, and then not wanting to take any chances of running head-on into the posse, hastily backtracked to where he could cut away and there pointed the sorrel south. He was reasonably sure that his activities would keep Huckaby and his posse puzzling over the trail for some time and thus leave him free to search the Mescal country for Lynch.

Free. The word evoked a strange feeling within him. This breaking away, this eluding of Virgil Huckaby and the law he represented, placed him in the same category as Mason Lynch; now they were both outlawed. He shrugged. It was a situation that had been forced upon him, and with a man's life at stake, he had no regrets.

He had not noticed but it had grown lighter. A pale flare filled the heavens to the east and the stars were beginning to fade. Not long until sunrise. He would be reaching the country where he could expect to find Mason at about the right time.

Mason would not have covered much ground despite the several hours start that he had. His horse was in no condition for a hard, fast ride, and thinking it over, Shawn concluded his best bet was to move south as quickly as possible, get near the Mescals, and then backtrack, work his way north. In so doing. and assuming he had figured right and Mason was heading for his ranch, he could expect to encounter the man.

He wondered what Mason would find at his ranch. Apparently he had only begun its building when the war came and he rode out to fight. Those four years, plus the succeeding ten he had spent in prison, added up to a period that could have nullified and completely erased all the effort he had put into the property.

Starbuck hoped it would prove otherwise. Lynch was a man desperately seeking haven, a refuge from a life that had not been kind. And now he was opening a new and tragic chapter. Whether he had been the one who murdered Kit Canfield or not was a situation that should be faced squarely and settled.

Mason must be made to realize that. There was no future whatsoever for him if he elected to avoid the confrontation, decided to run, hide from the law and those pseudo-lawmen, the bounty hunters who would come swarming in as soon as the reward Barney Canfield most certainly would post, was noised about.

No man could find fulfillment in a life forever peopled by threatening shadows; Mason Lynch should understand that, and if innocent, take steps to clear his name. But if he were guilty, if he had been the one who killed Canfield, then—Starbuck shrugged, not liking the question that thought raised.

The law declared a man must be made to face up to his crimes; could he, by force if necessary, capture and take Mason Lynch in for that purpose? Must he personally assume what would be a most disagreeable obligation? Mason was a beaten man, one scarred cruelly by life, but the law was the guideline to which all must adhere and to which there can be no exceptions. He hoped he would not be forced to make any such decision.

An hour later he broke out into a land of rolling ridges covered with gently waving grass, sage-filled draws, and small oases of cottonwoods and other trees. A stream sparkled along the floor of a vast, far-flung valley, and at its far end he saw the rambling formations he assumed to be the Mescal Mountains.

Dismounting, he picketed the sorrel in a small clearing and made his way to a shoulder of rock thrusting itself, like a thick shelf, into the swale and affording a lofty and excellent vantage point from which to observe. He was about midway of the basin, he judged, looking to both directions, and should be well below the slower-traveling Mason—between him and the Mescals—*if he had been right*. He had only guessed that Lynch would choose this route; he could be wrong.

But he was confident that he had read the man's mind correctly. Mason, in reality, had no choice when you came right down to it; a slow horse and caught near dead center of the territory, the logical answer would be the Mescals, where, on his own land, he could lie low until the horse had recovered and it was safe to move on.

Fixing his eyes on the southernmost point of the valley visible to him, Shawn began a methodic search along the stream until he found the trail he knew would be there. In this land, not too great a distance now from the desert, travelers, both man and beast, never strayed far from water in their migrations. To do so invited hardship, occasionally even death.

Slowly, painstakingly, Starbuck began to trace the course of the creek with its complementing path, following it with his eyes as it wound in and out of the trees, through the brush, now and again in the open where it became a silver ribbon glinting brightly in the sunlight.

Halfway across a narrow flat, movement arrested his attention. He came to his feet slowly, squinting to concentrate his vision as well as cut down the glare—and then settled back as a doe mule deer walked leisurely out of the brush, paused to survey the surrounding area for possible enemies while testing the breeze with her nostrils. Reassured, she meandered on down to the water, head bobbing rhythmically with each graceful step.

Suddenly the doe came to a rigid alert. A shift in the light breeze had apparently carried a warning to her. Starbuck edged farther out on the ledge, probed the country above the poised animal with a careful gaze.

He saw then what had startled the animal. It was Mason Lynch, again on foot and leading his horse, making his way along the stream.

For a considerable length of time Starbuck studied Lynch's slow progress along the trail. Then, fixing in his mind the location of a rock bench well ahead of the man where an interception could be made, he returned to the sorrel, mounted and rode down the slope.

He reached the foot of the long grade without incident. Keeping above and back from the creek, he made his way to the overhanging slab of granite he had selected and halted. There again picketing the gelding but this time with greater care, he crawled to the extreme lip of the ledge. From that elevated position he could look down upon the stream and its adjacent trail as well as observe anyone approaching from all directions.

He would be above Mason's line of vision, and that assured him. There was no way of anticipating the man's reaction, now that he was a fugitive, faced possibly with a death sentence or at the least the promise of spending the remainder of his life behind prison walls. And a man once considered a friend could now be an enemy in his eyes; therefore, it was only prudent to proceed with caution.

Flat on the gray-streaked rock bench, Shawn held his gaze to the upper end of the trail, awaited the initial appearance of Mason Lynch. The sun was out and well on its way across the clean sky by that moment, and already was making its searing presence felt. Jays flitted about in the scrubby pinons and cedars, their crests lifting and falling as they scolded lesser birds, warning them from their asserted territory; high overhead a Mexican eagle soared in ever-extending circles as it hunted from an exalted level.

Insects buzzed noisily in the weedy growth struggling for life from the crevices in the rock, and a gopher, frightened into hiding by the arrival of the sorrel and his rider, satisfied finally that all now was well since he could detect no more sound or movement, reappeared, scurried up onto the lower lip of the shelf, where he rose to a rigid, military stance while he studied the land below with bright, sharp eyes.

Shawn stirred restlessly, loosened the bandanna around his neck. The heat was beginning to drill into him, reach the inner depths of his body. Mason should be close, he thought, but judging distance from an overhead position can be difficult and quite often unreliable. Lynch might have been farther away than he figured.

Impatiently, Starbuck brushed at the sweat accumulating on his face. He'd be glad when this was all over and done with, settled one way or another. Then he could go on about his business—that of looking up a rider named Ivory at Canfield's Box C and determining whether he was his missing brother, Ben, or not. That was what had brought him down into Arizona Territory in the first place, but it seemed he was always getting sidetracked—involved. . . .

The minutes dragged by. Another quarter-hour—a half. Again Shawn stirred, the direct, blazing shafts of sunlight bearing down mercilessly. The gopher, startled for the third time, darted away, disappeared into the loose rocks. The eagle had drifted on seeking more productive hunting, but the jays were still there—quarrelsome, noisy, and impertinent.

A blur of motion up-trail—Starbuck's attention focused on the point instantly. It was Lynch. He was rounding a clump of brush, hat in hand, the bay following and not limping to any great extent. Apparently Mason was permitting the horse to take it easy, saving him in the event sudden and hard use should become necessary. A pistol was thrust under Lynch's waistband, the butt sticking out at a handy angle.

Shawn remained motionless, ignoring the pesky, buzzing flies that circled his head, seeking to light on his sweaty skin. Motion, however small, could catch Mason's eyes, tip him off and seriously complicate the situation.

Looking close, Starbuck endeavored to judge the frame of mind dominating the man. He was running a great personal risk, he realized, no matter how he made his presence known. At the first sound of a voice or the small move of anything, Mason likely would react violently. His nerves would be at hair-trigger keenness and likely he would shoot blindly and without thought.

It would be wise to act when the man was still in front

89

of him and not after he had passed the ledge, Shawn decided. There was at least a chance that Lynch would recognize him in that split second before he pulled the trigger of his weapon.

Mason drew near, became definite. Sweat lay thick on his forehead and cheeks, glistened in his neck and arms. His shirt was soaked, long, dark streaks running down from his armpits, extending across his shoulders. Weariness lined his face and rode him like a leaden pack that threatened to bring him to his knees. There was no spring in his step, only a mechanical trudging, a placing of one foot ahead of the other. He'd had a hard time of it during the night and there was little strength remaining in his tortured body.

He came to a listless, sliding halt. Ground-reining the bay, he looked ahead to the now hazy tumble of the Mescals, then turned, walked slowly down to the stream. Kneeling, he dashed water over his head, against his burned face, and then dripping, sat for a time hunched on his heels, resting. But it was for only brief minutes. Rising, he glanced to the sky as if searching for relief from the pitiless heat, and finding no hope, moved back to the bay. Catching up the trailing leathers, he resumed his jaded march.

Off behind Starbuck the sorrel, annoyed by the hordes of ravenous insects, shook itself violently. Instantly Mason Lynch stopped, hand going straight to the pistol at his waist.

Shawn, flattened upon the ledge as much as possible, felt rather than saw the man's sharp eyes digging at the rocks, the slope beyond him. If the sorrel moved again the moment of resolution was at hand; if not, likely Mason, seeing nothing and hearing no more, would assume it had been some animal frightened by his approach, and move on.

The charged, blistering moments crawled by filled with the dry clacking of insects, the drone of flies hovering above his sweaty skin. He dared not raise his head to see if Mason had dismissed the alarm and was continuing his passage, feared to stir at all since Lynch could still be scanning the rock ledges and slopes for the source of the noise.

A full, interminable minute . . . two . . . three. Shawn heard the click of metal against stone, swallowed hard. Mason was again on his way—almost directly below him if he could judge by the nearness of the sound. With great care he lifted his head a few inches. Lynch was a dozen steps away.

Starbuck reached for his pistol, drew it slowly, carefully, making certain it did not scrape against the rock. Second thoughts entered his mind. He decided against the procedure, slid the weapon back into its holster. Best to face Mason with both hands clearly visible—and empty.

Drawing his legs up beneath him, balancing himself with palms flat against the blistering granite, he waited until Lynch was coming straight toward him. Then, taking a deep breath, he rose to his full height.

"Mason—"

Lynch jolted as if struck bodily by the solitary word. He threw himself back against his horse, fingers clawing for the gun in the waistband of his pants.

"It's me—Starbuck!"

At the mention of the name Lynch froze. His hand drifted away from his weapon as he saw none in Shawn's grasp. Slowly he straightened, brushing at the sweat clothing his eyes with a forearm.

"You stood a damn good chance of getting your head blowed off."

"I know that. A risk I had to take," Starbuck said, keeping his arms away from his sides.

Mason considered him suspiciously. "You come after me?"

Shawn moved nearer to the edge of the shelf. "Not exactly—not after you."

Lynch shook his head. "Wasted your time. How'd you know to come this way?"

"Remembered what you said about the Mescals—that you'd once started to build yourself a ranch there. Sort of guessed that was where you'd make for."

The tautness still held Mason Lynch in a viselike grip. "I can forget that, I reckon," he said in a low, disconsolate voice. "They'd never leave me be. Was aiming to rest my horse till morning, then hit for the border. Ain't too far from here."

"One night won't do him much good for that kind of a trip. Must be a hundred miles across there. You sure that's what you want to do?"

Mason shrugged indifferently. "Nothing else left."

"Could be. You shoot Kit Canfield?"

Lynch laughed, a harsh, grating sound. "There anybody thinks I didn't?"

Far back up the slope above Starbuck a rock clattered hollowly, set up a thumping sound as it started downgrade.

Instantly Mason's mouth snapped shut. His hand reached again for the pistol in his waistband. Starbuck spun, threw his glance to the outcropping on the crest where he had earlier stopped and shortly thereafter spotted Mason.

A dozen riders were outlined against the sky. One man, on foot, was crouched at the extreme edge of the rocky shoulder, staring down the long slope into the valley. That would be the Indian, Yaqui Joe—the tracker. He hadn't succeeded in throwing the posse off for long, Shawn realized.

He came back around, met Mason Lynch's hard, accusing eyes, saw the leveled pistol pointing at him.

"Something I never figured from you—leading them to where I'd be."

"That's not the way of it," Shawn said quietly. "They're following me—not you. Thought I'd shaken them, but they've got themselves a tracker—Yaqui Joe they called him. He must've figured what I was doing first off. Hoped I'd have a couple hours' start on them at least."

Mason Lynch only stared, his red-lidded eyes sunk deep in his pinched face.

"It's the truth. If I was leading them I would've stuck with them. Makes more sense. Fact is, I was supposed to do just that but I ducked out, came on alone."

"So's you could escort me across the border, that it?"

Shawn ignored the thick sarcasm. "Nope, to get you out of the way before that posse could catch up. Huckaby's at the head of it but they're mostly Canfield lovers, and I don't figure the marshal will be able to hold them back if they ever get their hands on you. There's only one thing on their minds—string you up."

"Them wanting to do that is nothing new."

Starbuck looked up slope again. "Well, it's what you can figure on if we keep standing here. They'll find where I came off the rim, follow my tracks—and the next thing you know they'll be right in our laps."

Mason did not lower his weapon, simply continued to stand rigidly in the blazing sun. "Could all be a double-cross . . . a trick. Maybe there's more of them circling around us. For all I know you're working right with Huckaby and Canfield."

Starbuck swore in disgust. "I'm working for nobody but myself—and, I guess, sort of for you. And why I'm doing that even I'm not sure! It's your trouble, not mine—your neck they're wanting to stretch. Hell, if I had a lick of sense I'd climb on my horse and ride out, let you handle your own problems."

92

"You're not about to—not with me holding this gun on you!"

"I don't think you'd shoot me, Mason—and if you did pull that trigger you'd have Huckaby and his bunch down on you before you could get a half-mile. Use your head. I'm trying to help you—trying to be your friend!"

Mason continued to stare at Shawn for another long, silent minute, and then his arm began to lower. Shifting wearily, he thrust the weapon into his waistband.

"All right," he said in a resigned voice. "I'm leaving it up to you. What'll I do now?"

15

Relief flooded through Starbuck, broke the iron-hard tension that gripped him. He wiped at the sweat on his forehead, cast another glance to the rim above them. Huckaby's riders were still there but he could no longer see Yaqui Joe. That could only mean the canny old Indian was back somewhere on the plateau, nosing about for prints that would tell him where the sorrel started down. He would locate them with little difficulty, and soon the posse would come racing down the grade.

"Got to pull out of here quick," he said, wheeling toward the thicket where the sorrel waited. "Be smart, I think, to double back upstream."

Mason made no reply, held off until Starbuck had led his horse off the bench and down to the level of the trail.

"The way I just come?" he said. "Why not keep going for the border?"

"Be what they'll figure you'd do. We cut north, stay in the stream so's there'll be no tracks, and it ought to throw them off us in a hurry. Even that Indian can't pick up hoofprints there. Got to be careful, however. Couple of places where the water's out in the open. See us easy, if they're looking."

"They're starting down now," Mason said.

That would mean that Yaqui Joe had found the point where he'd begun the descent from the plateau. He'd hoped to have time in which to brush out the tracks both he and Lynch had made in the immediate area, but it was too late now.

Leading the way, he waded into the shin-deep stream at a fast walk with the sorrel slogging in behind him, sending up sprays of water from his hoofs at each step. He could hear Mason Lynch and the bay keeping pace.

For a good quarter-mile he maintained a steady gait,

94

working up a sweat despite the cool surroundings. Finally, with breath coming hard from the sheer labor of not only bucking the current but from the continually lifting grade as well, he halted in a wide bend of the creek. There a thick covering of cottonwood branches completely sheltered them from any possibility of being seen.

Climbing out onto the bank, water dripping from his soaked pant legs where the sorrel had splashed him, he tied the horse to a clump of birch and sat down upon a rotting log. Pulling off his boots, he poured the collected water from them, then, stripping off his socks, he wrung them dry and hung them on a nearby bush. A short distance away, Mason Lynch, close-mouthed and morose, was following the same procedure.

When those necessary creature-comfort chores were completed and both had settled back to regain spent breath and ease their aching muscles, Lynch finally turned to Starbuck. The dark void of bitterness, of utter hopelessness in the man's eyes Shawn had noticed at their first meeting, had returned, and there was a conspicuous drag to his voice.

"Now what? Got them between me and the border—and I'd be a fool to keep riding north. Thinking on it, seems I've been herded around to where I'm between a high fence and a tall place."

Angered, Starbuck shook his head. "If you figure me for some kind of a Judas-goat, then climb on my horse and head out. He'll get you away from here fast—"

"I'm not saying—"

"Then quit thinking it. Just be damned glad you're hid. That's a lynch mob back there."

Mason shrugged. "I expected it to be. You say Huckaby's running it?"

"Supposed to be, but the way Barney Canfield's got the men all fired up—offering a hundred dollars gold for you, dead or alive—I don't think the marshal can stop them if they ever get a hold of you, start in."

"Doubt if he'll even try."

Shawn nodded slowly. "Got to admit that I'm not so sure of him either. Thought all along he was trying to do a job, now I'm wondering about it. You've never got around to answering my question."

"What was that?"

"Kit Canfield—you shoot him? Tell the truth, Mason. A lie will only make it harder to help."

Lynch's eyes locked with those of Starbuck, held. "It wasn't me," he said soberly. "That's the God's truth. I was

95

there—I'm admitting that—but I didn't have anything to do with the shooting."

Starbuck leaned forward. "You saw it?"

"I was about as far from Kit as we are from that big rock—fifteen, maybe twenty strides."

"Then you recognized the man who did it?"

"Seen a man—that's about all. Never got a clear look at him."

Shawn settled back despondently. "Not much there that'll help."

"What I told myself when it was all over and I was standing there in the dark. Who'd believe a yarn like that from me? Everybody knows how things stood between me and the Canfields—and a lot of them are dead sure I came back to square up with the other two. You saw that."

Starbuck's eyes were thoughtful. "How was it that you just happened to be right there?"

Mason's eyes spread slightly and then his head came forward as his shoulders sagged. "You're proving my point. You don't believe a goddam word I'm saying. It's a cinch Huckaby and everybody else'll look at it the same way."

"Not saying I don't. Let's hear the rest of it."

Mason lifted his hands, allowed them to drop to his sides in a gesture of hopelessness. "What for? Won't do no good. Either you believe me—or you don't."

"Wrong!" Shawn snapped. "You've got to convince folks and the best way to do that is start with me—a friend. Then we can work together at making somebody like Huckaby listen—maybe even Barney Canfield, if we can get close enough to him."

"Not sure there's any use trying to talk to any of them."

"We'll go to Tucson, then, lay it out for him. But the thing now is let me hear all of it—everything that went on. Just give up, keep feeling sorry for yourself and how you're going to have to spend the rest of your life dodging the law—and there'll be nothing for me to do but move on, tend to my own business."

Mason's gaunt face had tipped down. His eyes were set, staring, reflected his hopelessness. "Probably be best anyway, Shawn. All I can do is cause you grief—maybe even get you shot."

"Something for me to decide."

"You standing by me, being a friend—that's the best thing that's happened to me in a lot of years. Thinking you'd changed, brought that posse down on me, sort of

96

jolted something inside me—and then if you don't believe—"

"The rest of it," Starbuck broke in gently. "Let me hear it."

Mason shifted, brushed at his lips. He sighed deeply, picked up a twig lying at his feet, began to snap it into small lengths.

"Went down to the graveyard after I left you last night," he began. "Had a look at the folks' graves, done some weed pulling and straightening up, then I got to thinking about Marie—she's the one I told you about."

Shawn nodded. "The one you'd figured to marry."

"I was remembering what you said," Lynch went on in a wooden voice as if not hearing, "and decided I would like to see her, maybe talk to her. Thought she might have some feeling for me—that maybe there was still a chance we could sort of get together, team up.

"Her being what the marshal said she was and all that don't make no difference to me. When I studied on it I could see it was my fault she ended up that way. Besides, I ain't got much to offer either—a busted-down convict with nothing more'n a piece of land.

"Well, I went down to the Frisco House and was standing there looking through the window at her and a couple others, trying to get up enough guts to go in, when Kit Canfield came along. I watched him go inside, like he owned the place, and got right after Marie. He took her upstairs—and I know I've got no right, but it riled me plenty."

"You go in then, make something of that?" Starbuck asked hurriedly. There had been some remark to the effect that Lynch had been seen; he wasn't exactly certain of the details.

"Nope—just stood around outside. Wasn't sure what I wanted to do—or could do, not knowing how Marie would feel. I was still hanging around when Kit came out, couple hours later."

"Anybody else show up around there?"

"Not that I saw. Once I thought I heard somebody walking in the road, coming from town, but I never did see who it was. Anyway, Kit came out, started across the street for the old stable where he'd left his horse."

"That was when the man you say killed him showed up?"

Mason smiled tiredly, wagged his head. Starbuck, catching the unfortunate way he had phrased the words, said:

"Don't take that as meaning I don't believe you—it was just how it sounded."

"Sure, sure," Lynch murmured. "Fellow came out of the stable. Guess he must've been in there all the time, or maybe he was who I heard on the road. He walked out into the middle of the street and met Kit. They just seemed to be talking. Then I hear a shot, all sort of muffled, like when you cover a gun with a blanket or something and pull the trigger. Kit just stood there for a few seconds, then fell.

"The man turned and ducked back into the stable. I guess I was a little surprised or something, and I wasn't hankering to get mixed up in it, so I didn't do anything, just stood there for a little bit. Then I finally went out to where Kit was laying. He was dead."

"Shot with his own pistol," Shawn said. "They found it under him."

Lynch swore, recognizing the implication immediately. "Guess that's the cincher for a lot of folks—them that knew I wasn't carrying a gun."

Shawn made no reply. Mason, head bowed, tossed the broken bits of the twig aside one by one, said: "Came to me right then that people'd all figure it was me who did it because of the trouble I've had with the Canfields, and that I might as well forget trying to start over again."

"Didn't you go into the stable looking for the man who did it?"

"No point. Heard him riding off about the time I was looking at Kit. Headed west, it seemed."

"West?" Starbuck asked, frowning. "What's in that direction?"

"Not much—leastwise there didn't use to be. Things could've changed since I was there last but once there was only the folks' place—Canfield's now—and the road that hooks up with the one going to California."

"Somebody figuring to head out that way would've had to get himself all set—grub, water and the like. No towns for a lot of miles. You get any look at all at the killer?"

Mason shook his head. "Too dark. Couldn't see his face at all."

"Was he dressed any special way?"

"Regular cowhand clothes, I reckon. Did notice he wore some kind of a checked vest."

"Was it a plaid shirt?" Starbuck asked quickly, remembering that Marshal Virgil Huckaby had been wearing such a garment.

"Could've been," Lynch said, not making the connection. "Like I told you, it was hard to tell much about anything."

Shawn considered what Mason had said. There was indeed very little to go on; only one thing could have meaning—the checked vest or shirt being worn by the killer. Such were common but not necessarily plentiful. They had that and the belief that the man had ridden west after the murder.

"What happened then?"

"Somebody yelled in the street. The shot had been heard inside the house, too. I looked, saw a man bending over Kit, and another one coming through the yard. Right then I decided the best thing I could do was get my horse and leave town fast—try to make it across the border into Mexico. Was plain to me I'd have a hell of a time getting anybody to believe it wasn't me who done the shooting."

"Probably be harder than you think," Starbuck said. "You were seen standing there in the doorway of the stable. One of the women from the house. Says she didn't know the man she saw but that she could recognize him if she ever saw him again."

Mason swore raggedly. "You see? What's the use? Man can't buck a stacked deck!" He looked up, faced Shawn squarely. "One thing I'd like to know—you've heard my side of it, where do you stand? You believing me or not?"

"I believe you," Starbuck said without hesitation. "Thought all along that killing was something you'd not let yourself in for—not after spending ten years behind prison walls for one. Kept thinking, too, about the way you felt over being free and having your own place."

Lynch sighed. "Makes a difference to me. I'm obliged to you. Wish there was more I could tell you about that killer. Ain't much there to go on."

"Enough—maybe. A man in a plaid shirt or vest, and the fact that he rode out of town, going west—that's a little something. Thing we've got to decide is what we ought to do next."

"Plenty clear what I'd best do," Lynch said glumly. "Only way I can keep my neck from getting stretched is leave the country, like I was planning to do."

"Give up everything you want—your place in the Mescals? That girl—Marie?"

"Not much chance of seeing either one again, way things are lined up. Barney Canfield, big as he is and pushing Huckaby around like he does—and that woman seeing me there—hell, I'd be a fool to risk staying around. If you're honest with me, you'll admit I'm right."

"Maybe, but I don't like to see you just up and quit. If we could get some kind of an idea who the killer was, by tracking maybe, could be we could come up with something we could tell the law."

"Not Huckaby—be a waste of time. I don't trust him."

Starbuck was silent for a while, then: "Not sure I do either. Few things about him that's got me wondering, but we'll not bother with him—not yet anyway. If we can turn up something, we can ride to Tucson, talk to the sheriff there."

"I don't know," Mason said slowly, growing colder to the idea. "Lawmen sort of hang together. Nothing says he wouldn't clap me in a cell and send for Huckaby."

"Not if we had something solid to tell him, give him to work on."

Mason frowned, interest picking up. "You think we can make something of what I told you?"

"Have to. It's all we've got."

Lynch reached for his now dry socks, began to pull them on. There was a briskness to his movements that bespoke the hope stirring within him.

"Know that country west of town. Grew up roaming all through it—hunting and such. I'm remembering a few places where a man could hole up for a spell."

Shawn studied Mason Lynch for a few moments as he began to draw on his footwear. He had built up that hope in the man, was now wondering if he could deliver; there was so little to go on!

"No doubt in your mind the killer rode west?"

"Sure as I know my name," Lynch replied. "You figure there'd be any use looking for tracks?"

"Doubt it," Starbuck said, rising and stamping into his boots. "Never find the right ones along the edge of town. Too many riders coming and going. Might get lucky but I sure would hate to bank on it."

"Expect that's going to be the whole story," Mason said soberly. He was standing off to the side, his features bleak, voice lifeless. "Could all be for nothing—like shooting at the moon. With my kind of luck, we'll likely come up with a flat nothing."

"Maybe so," Shawn murmured, "but we've got to try."

Mason Lynch raised his head, glanced at Starbuck. A grudging smile parted his lips. "I reckon we do," he said, and moved toward his horse.

16

Keeping to the creek until they reached a wider, well-graveled area, Shawn guided the sorrel out into the shallows, halted. Mason drew up beside him.

"Something wrong?"

"Looking for the tracks you made when you came down this way."

Lynch raised himself in his stirrups, gazed around thoughtfully. "Be over there—by that gooseberry patch. Recollect walking by it."

Starbuck scrubbed at the sweat on his face. "Like to get over there to them without making any new ones. That Indian Huckaby's got will be hard to fool. More we mix things up, the better."

Mason glanced downstream. "We've been in the water for quite a ways. He sure won't find tracks there."

"That's how we want to keep it," Shawn said, and touching the sorrel with his spurs, angled for the trail.

"Could go right through them gooseberries," Lynch said as they broke out onto dry ground. "He won't find no tracks in them."

"No tracks but there'd be plenty of broken branches and mashed leaves that we couldn't fix. No job to cut a switch and brush out the prints we're leaving now."

Mason nodded. "Guess you're right . . . What are you aiming to do, backtrack my trail?"

"Best thing. The Indian may never get upstream this far, but if he does, I want everything plenty confused."

"He'll puzzle it out—see how I came down alone, then went back up with somebody else—and they'll guess that somebody else's you."

"Maybe, but it'll take time—and that's something we need a lot of."

They reached the berry thicket, swung onto the faint path bordering its east side, halted.

"Stay in the saddle," Shawn directed, dropping to the ground. "This'll only take a couple of minutes, and the fewer tracks we have to cover, the better."

Thrusting a hand into a boot, he drew the keen-bladed knife he carried in a stitched-in leather sheath, cut a thickly leafed branch from the back side of a gooseberry clump. Doubling back to the edge of the shallow water, he carefully swept out the prints the horses had made, pausing now and then to sift a bit of loose dirt and litter over the places that appeared to have been disturbed.

Then, once again on the gelding, he resumed the trail, keeping exactly to the line taken by Lynch when he came down into the valley. One good thing, he noted, was that the soil was firm on the long grade, being a type of solidly packed sod in which a tough, narrow-bladed glass grew. Trailing them, if the Yaqui managed to get to this point, would not be easy.

But he knew better than to sell the tracker short, and as they wound their way toward the plateau lying north of the valley, he was continually taking precautions, doing everything possible to cover signs of their passage.

Sometime before noon, with the sun blazing down in unabated strength, they climbed out of the basin and found themselves on fairly level ground. Pulling into the shade of a scatter of pines, they dismounted, easing their own sweaty bodies as well as resting the sorrel and the ailing bay, whose condition was steadily worsening. But there was no time to spare and within a half-hour they were again in the saddle, riding due west, challenging the hot wind that now was blowing in from the distant desert.

Little conversation passed between them, only an occasional and necessary comment as each man, wrapped in his own thoughts, felt inclined to keep his peace. Starbuck, for himself, was again thinking of his purpose for being in the Rockinstraw Valley country—that of looking up the man called Jim Ivory, and discussing, hopefully, the possibility of him being his long absent brother Ben.

It irritated him to become sidetracked when following out a good and definite lead, not only because of time lost but because it brought about another complication, money. The small amount of cash granted him by the lawyer handling old Hiram Starbuck's estate had long since run out, and it was now a matter of halting the quest at intervals while he took a job—one of cowhand, deputy marshal, stagecoach driver, or shotgun guard—anything available if it paid hard cash—long enough for him to accumulate sufficient funds to see him through a few more months.

He was about to that low point now where the necessity for finding temporary work would be the next thing in order. If Jim Ivory proved to be Ben, then there would be no problem; if not, he'd ride on—to Las Cruces, perhaps. There was a sheriff there, according to Virg Huckaby, who was looking for a man trained as a boxer—a boxer who might be Ben. As well look for a job there and find out more about—

"That cabin—in the clearing—"

Mason Lynch's voice cut into his thoughts. He roused, looked to the direction in which the man pointed.

"It's one of the places I figured the killer might use as a hideout."

Starbuck, a little surprised at having reached the area so quickly, swung in behind a clump of oak, eyed the sagging, weathered structure.

"Old prospector, name of Tait, used to live there. Was a friend of my folks, more or less—his kind don't ever get too friendly. Apaches killed him."

"Raid?" Shawn asked, wondering why the structure had not been burned to its rock foundation.

"Nope, wasn't that. Tait caught himself a young Apache gal, somehow, kept her tied up inside the place so's he'd have a woman for himself. Got by with it for a whole winter, then a party of braves, still hunting for her, I reckon, found her.

"They hid out in the cabin and when Tait come in that evening about dark from working his claim, they jumped him. Spread-eagled him to the wall, then stood back and threw knives and tomahawks at him. Finished him off by shooting him full of arrows.

"Killed the squaw, too, only they done it quick, didn't make her suffer like they did him. Took me a long time to understand why they killed her—her being their own kind and all. Pa said it was because she'd been a white man's woman—it not making any difference whether she wanted to be or not."

"Probably the answer," Starbuck said. "But it could've been that Tait had come to mean something to her, and she tried to help him. They'd lived together for a whole winter. Seems kind of strange she couldn't have got away from him during all that time."

"Is sort of funny," Mason said. "My pa was the one who found them. Buried them back there in those trees.

103

Can't remember all the details—only what Pa told me—and that was in private. Ma wouldn't stand for such being talked about in front of her. They were both heathens, according to the way she looked at it."

Shawn continued to study the weathered structure. After a bit he shook his head. "Don't think there's anybody using that place. Ground's not chopped up like it would be if there was a horse coming and going. Best we be sure, though. You stay here, keep me covered. I'll circle around, come in from the hind side."

Swinging away, Starbuck followed the thick brush that fringed the clearing, pulled up shortly in a small grove directly behind the cabin. It was in worse condition, at closer range, than it had appeared at first look. That someone could be living inside seemed most unlikely.

Tying the gelding to a stout cedar, he drew his forty-five, moved quietly around the north side of the hut, and came in to the front. There were a few hoof indentations in the grass-covered sod, but all were old. Nowhere did he see any droppings.

Crossing to the partly open door, he stopped, looked down. Dust had accumulated thick on the sill; it was unsullied except for the tracks of packrats and field mice. Holstering his weapon, he placed a hand against the ax-fashioned slab, shoved it aside, and stepped into the gloomy, stale-smelling room.

A double-width bunk had been built against the wall directly in front of him. Gray ashes in the rock fireplace was proof of occupancy by some drifter or possibly working cowhand, seeking shelter from a winter storm—but they were months old, perhaps over a year. Turning, Shawn stepped out into the open, signaled to Mason Lynch, and retraced his steps to the sorrel.

"Been a long time since anybody was in there," he said as they rode on. "Any other old cabins or line shacks around?"

"Not that I remember," Mason said, his voice reflecting the disappointment he felt in not finding any evidence that could lead to the killer. "Some caves over in the next canyon."

"Big enough for a man to camp in?"

Mason nodded. "Indians once did. Sort of like cliff dwellings."

Shawn remembered such an area up in northern New Mexico, and a larger settlement farther to the west on the Colorado border; sheer embankments with living quarters gouged out of the face.

"A whole village?"

"No, nothing like that. Just a couple of caves. Probably one family driven off by the tribe, crawled in and stayed a while. Or it could've been a small party hiding from others."

The caves, no more extensive than Mason had indicated, proved as fruitless as the prospector's old cabin. The sole tenants, according to all evidence, were a pair of coyotes.

The effect it had upon Mason Lynch was immediately apparent. The bitterness in his eyes became more pronounced and a sort of surly indifference possessed him. Squatting on his haunches, toying with a palm full of sand, he muttered a curse, said: "Reckon that lays it out plain."

Shawn considered the man quietly, fully aware of the change. "Meaning what?"

"I'd be a damned fool to hang around now. I'd best be lining out for the border."

"What about the plan we set up—that of us trying to run down the rider you heard heading west?"

"Figured we'd find some trace of him—but I should've known there'd be no trace. Hell, what's the use!"

Mason raised his arm, slammed the grains of sand he held to the ground. "Nothing—never a goddam thing—works out right for me! You got to admit it."

"Only thing I'll admit is that we haven't given it a chance—our searching around, I mean. Now, if you'll feel better about it, why not hole up somewhere for a spell and let me do the looking. Or, if you'll willing to trust Huckaby, I'll wait until the posse goes back to town, slip in and have a talk with him. Maybe, after I tell him what you saw—"

"Forget it," Mason said flatly. "He'd not believe you, and about the first thing he'd do would be to lock you up for tricking him. One answer, far as I can see, and that's for me to get the hell out of this goddam country. Been nothing but a jinx to me!"

"Be a mistake to quit now, Mason—and I can't let you do it."

"You've got nothing to say about it," Lynch snapped, coming to his feet abruptly, pistol in his hand. Pain filled his eyes and there was almost apology in his voice. "Hell of a note when a man has to throw down on the best friend he's got—but it's the only thing I can do."

Starbuck stared, wagged his head slowly. "Never figured you'd turn on me—"

"For your own good. You hang around with me and my kind of luck'll rub off on you. That sorrel of yours, reckon I'll have to borrow him. Bay'll never make it—but don't worry, I'll treat him right and you'll get him back. I'll leave him in the stable at San Miguel—town just across the border. You'll be fine on the bay. Just ride straight on. The Box C's just over that ridge ahead."

Taut, angry, Shawn faced Mason Lynch. "Happens this is all your trouble, not mine," he said, rising slowly. "I'm trying to help you—not myself. Can't you get that in your head?"

"Wasting your time. You ought to've realized that by now. Thing for me to do is cross the border, lose myself in Mexico."

"You won't ever lose the bounty hunters that'll be dogging your tracks. Canfield'll put up a big reward and it'll say dead or alive. You won't stand a chance."

"Sure as hell don't stand one around here!"

"How do you know? You keep blowing up every time things don't suit you—"

"It's more'n that," Lynch said hopelessly. "It's the way things always work out for me. Nothing ever pans out right, no matter what. Just seems I can't win."

"The hell you can't!" Shawn yelled, suddenly out of patience with the man. "The sooner you quit feeling sorry for yourself, the quicker we can get things straightened up! You've got a good chance of clearing your name, starting a new life, if you'll show some guts!"

"Sounds easy enough, coming from you, but I'm the one looking at a noose. Fact is, I'm the only one—"

"No, not the only one, maybe," Starbuck broke in. "I can name another one."

Mason stared. "Who?"

"Virg Huckaby."

Lynch's jaw sagged, then closed firmly. A frown narrowed his eyes. "You handing me a line of bull? You saying that just to—"

"Stop and think. Huckaby hated Kit Canfield plenty, maybe more than anybody around—even you. Big reason is that he stands to lose his job as marshal, and that means a lot to him—everything, I'd say. He could quit worrying about it if Canfield was dead. Now, what was it you said about the shirt the killer was wearing?"

"It was checked . . ."

"Now think back to Huckaby—when you last saw him. What kind of a shirt was he wearing?"

"By God!" Lynch exclaimed, jamming his pistol back

into its place. "Virg was wearing a checked shirt!" Opening a hand, he smashed his fist into the palm. "Dammit—I wish't I could remember for sure what that killer had on. Ain't sure if it was a vest or a shirt. But checked, I know that. Maybe black and white—or it could've been red and white."

"It's something we've got to go on—and maybe even gives us a good suspect," Starbuck said. "Whole thing it proves is that you'd be a fool to run."

"Maybe," Lynch murmured, again wavering.

"No maybe to it. You do what you are thinking and it'll be worse than the ten years you spent in the pen. Man doesn't need high walls to be in prison; he can build one for himself simply by trying to hide—dodge the lawmen, the bounty hunters—the friends that hear about the reward—"

Shawn broke off suddenly, lifted his hand as the hard pound of a fast-running horse cut through the hush lying over the heated land. Rising, he crossed to where Mason stood, and together they looked down into the shallow basin where the trail continued on westward.

A lone rider—apparently heading for the Box C. The man rounded a bend, for a brief time was faced toward them. Mason swore softly as surprise rocked Shawn Starbuck. It was Barney Canfield.

17

Starbuck considered the rancher in puzzled silence. Why had he pulled out, forsaken the posse at a time when it undoubtedly appeared to all they were closing in on their objective? Thinking back, he recalled that it had been Canfield himself who had forcefully made it clear to the men that no one was to quit until Mason Lynch had been brought down.

"Thought you said he was with Huckaby and that posse," Lynch murmured.

"He was—and I'm wondering why he pulled out. Him being here doesn't make sense."

"Heading for the ranch, that's for sure."

"Could be the posse's following," Shawn said, and glanced off toward the valley. "Nobody in sight, however."

"If they were coming, wouldn't he have waited, rode with them?"

"Seems—unless he had some special reason for wanting to be alone. Any way we can get to the Box C without taking the road he's on?"

Mason pointed to the ridge he had earlier indicated. "That's a bluff. You can look down on the place from there."

Immediately Starbuck turned to the sorrel, swung up, and moved off at a good clip. Lynch, on the bay, now showing a pronounced limp, fell in behind. By the time he reached the ridge, Shawn was already off his horse, and squatted on his heels, looked down from the crest of the steep butte at the Box C. Barney Canfield, sticking to the longer, more circuitous road that curved around the north end of the formation, was just coming into view.

"Not changed much," Lynch commented, hunkering next to Starbuck and scanning the scatter of buildings.

"They've built a few more sheds—a bigger barn—and added on to the bunkhouse. More corrals."

Starbuck's eyes noted the changes as Mason pointed them out, noticed, also, the thread of regret in the man's voice and wondered if the place meant as little to him as he professed. But it could be no more than memory; a man looking back on the old days, his early life, always recalls the good and the pleasant and experiences a twinge of longing.

"Biggest house, there in front—that's where we lived. Kitchen was at the end. Looks like the Canfields have put up a new one. My room was at the south end. I remember I'd get up early when I was a kid—earlier than I had to for chores—and stand by the window and watch the quail come down from the foothills going to water in our stock pond.

"Coveys would come regular as night follows day. Sometimes it would be a big bunch—maybe a hundred birds. Other times there'd be only twenty or thirty. Always tickled me when it was the time of year for chicks. I'd see the mother hen come along, running fast, looking like a fat old lady hurrying to church. The chicks would be strung out behind her in a line, their legs pumping like hell to keep up. Used to think of that a lot when I was laying out the nights in the pen. Sort of kept me from going out of my mind.

"That—that ironwood tree there by the corner of the house—planted it myself when I was hardly big enough to dig the hole. Brought it back one day from the desert. I'd gone there with Pa. Saw the big trees all covered with purple flowers, so I dug up a little one, brought it back as a present for Ma. Took a few years before it had any blossoms, but she liked it."

Shawn, listening to Mason Lynch, once again felt a prickle of doubt. That his folks' place did mean a great deal to the man was apparent now, despite his declarations to the contrary; it was evident in his voice, his manner, in the way his eyes were glowing. And the Canfields—the fact that he still refused to accept proof that a legitimate deal had been consummated between his parents and the three brothers—unquestionably were still the object of a fierce and burning hate on his part.

Starbuck stirred, deeply disturbed by his thoughts. He had been sure Mason was innocent, basing those convictions on his knowledge of the man and his own intuition. But he had been wrong before, he realized, and he could be again. Still . . .

He shifted his attention to the flat north of the ranch. Barney Canfield was just entering the high, square gate frame, his horse approaching the yard at a steady lope. The sound of thudding hooves brought the cook from the kitchen. An old man, he stood on the landing outside his work quarters, wiping his hands on what had once been a white apron but now was a darkly streaked gray, and awaited the rancher's arrival.

Another of the help, a Mexican, moved lazily out of the barn, and leaning on the hayfork with which he had evidently been working, also watched and waited.

Canfield pounded onto the hardpack, angled toward the cook. "George, got about a dozen men riding in for a bite to eat. It's that posse that's hunting Kit's killer. Ought to be here in maybe a half-hour, could be less. Get something ready for them."

"Sure thing, Mr. Canfield."

The rancher pulled away, rode on a short distance, and stopped again, this time at one of the corrals. The Mexican propped his fork against the side of the barn, ambled forward to look after the *patron's* horse. Dismounting, Barney asked a question of some sort of the man, who replied by pointing at the bunkhouse.

Something was happening—something that was important. Shawn could feel it. Canfield, it would seem, had ridden in ahead of Huckaby and the posse, which, unaccountably, was taking time out for lunch despite the rancher's previous insistence that there be no let-up in the search for Mason.

But, assuming hunger did get the best of the men and the break became necessary—why did Barney Canfield feel it necessary to leave the party himself on such a trivial errand as notifying the cook of their coming when he could have dispatched one of the hired hands accompanying him? And the need for such forewarning to the cook was hardly necessary, anyway; with a large crew such as the Box C would run, men would be coming and going at all hours. There would be plenty of food and hot coffee available at most any time.

A deep dissatisfaction possessed Shawn Starbuck. Too many things didn't add up. He turned to Lynch.

"There a way to get down there from here?"

"Trail over there to the left," Mason replied. "You can make it on foot—not with horses." He paused, stared at Shawn. "You aiming to go down?"

Shawn nodded.

"Don't see as how that can help any," Mason said,

110

doubt riding his voice. "With Huckaby and that posse about due, could be kind of a fool thing to try."

"Maybe, but we're looking for answers and it could be we'll find them there."

"And maybe I'll just be helping them put that rope around my neck—"

"No need for you to come. Wait here—just show me where that trail is."

Starbuck pulled back from the lip of the butte, came to his feet. More slowly, Mason took a place beside him, features drawn into a dark frown. Abruptly he shrugged.

"Hell—if you can keep from getting caught, reckon I can, too."

Starbuck nodded. "Hoped you'd come along. Likely be some things I'll need explained to me."

Lynch gave Shawn a quizzical look, cut off to his left, and kneeing his way into a stand of stiffly resisting snakeweed, bulled a path to where the rim of the bluff had broken off and slid into a steep draw.

Unhesitating, Mason dropped into it, began to descend, steadying and bracing himself on the slant by grasping the clumps of tough groundsel and rabbitbrush that grew out of the near-vertical sides. Shortly they were at the foot of the formation. The south end of the main house was no more than two dozen strides distant.

It was the blind side of the structure; a blanket had been hung over the window in the end—the same from which Mason had often watched the quail—and Shawn, hunched low, sprinted across the open ground to the forward corner of the building. Halting there, brushing at the sweat again covering his face, he waited until Lynch joined him.

He started to ask Mason about the arrangement of the remaining structures in relation to the yard, realized he would probably know very little about it; a number of new buildings and pens had been erected since he had last seen the place. Best find out for himself.

Quickly, he crossed to the opposite corner of the house, stopped, peered cautiously around the weather-smoothed stones toward the yard. He found little advantage as the new kitchen had been built only a few feet from the main structure, leaving only a narrow, separating breezeway which severally restricted any view of the hardpack and other buildings.

Taking a hurried survey of the cooking quarters, he saw the window in the wall facing him was high, served only for purposes of ventilation, and again bent low, ran forward until he had gained the opposite side of that more recently acquired structure.

A grunt of satisfaction came from him. An old corral, no longer in use, lay adjacent. To its right was the yard with all other buildings clearly visible. Still cautious, Shawn moved to the corral, crawled through a gap in the sagging crosspoles, and took up a position inside and to the front. He now had a complete view of the yard, could watch all activity with ease as well as hear any normal conversation that took place in the open without fear of being seen.

Lynch, lying beside him, brushed at his eyes nervously. "Somebody spots us—we'll be like trapped coyotes—"

"Stay low—nobody'll see us."

"You hope. Way my luck runs, we could get caught first thing. What're you looking for?"

Starbuck shrugged. "Anything—everything. I don't know. Just that I've got a feeling. May be a waste of time, but we've got to work from somewhere. One thing, when Virg Huckaby shows up, take a good look at that shirt he's wearing."

Shawn checked his whispered words, attention drawn to the Mexican hired hand coming from the interior of the barn again. Canfield had disappeared, going into the house, Starbuck supposed, and wondered if it would have been smarter to have found a place nearer that structure. He decided he was likely in as good a position as possible.

The hired hand circled the barn at an indifferent shuffle, returned shortly leading a chunky black gelding. Tethering him with a neck rope to the hitchrack fronting the bulky building, he went inside, reappeared dragging a saddle and other gear. With no effort at haste, he began to throw the equipment onto the black, all the while softly crooning some low-pitched south-of-the-border lament on love.

A door slammed loudly. The screen of the bunkhouse. A man appeared, saddlebags slung across one shoulder, a blanket roll trapped under an arm. Shawn felt Mason claw at his hand, turned. Lynch was staring at the rider.

"That's him—that's him! He's the one I seen shoot Kit!"

Starbuck came up instantly, swiveled his eyes to the man. He was stockily built, dark, walked with an easy swing. He was dressed much the same as any cowhand except that he sported a black-and-white-checked vest of the type designed for men with the less robust occupation of gambler; it was now much the worse for the hard, everyday use it was being subjected to.

112

"You sure?"

"Sure's I can be," Mason responded tensely. "It was dark but I ain't forgetting that fancy vest."

Shawn watched the man halt beside the black, hang his saddlebags over the skirt of the hull, anchor them, then affix the blanket roll atop the pouches. The Mexican lazed against the crossbar of the hitchrack.

"You ride, eh, *señor?*"

The squat man nodded. "Tired of this place, *amigo.*"

"You here for a long time. Where you go?"

"Mexico—maybe. You want to come along?"

"*Por Dios—no!* The *Federales,* they have look often for me. I do not wish for them to find me."

The rider laughed. "What'd you do—stick a *cuchillo* in one of those *señoritas* you're always singing about?"

"Maybe. It is a thing one does not speak of."

If this was the man who had slain Kit Canfield, what was he doing on the Canfield ranch? It appeared he was a regular hand and no stranger.

"Heading for Mexico—that proves it," Mason said in a low voice. "He's running."

"Looks like it. Any chance you're mistaken? Doesn't make much sense he'd be here—one of the hired help."

"Maybe it don't—but he's the one. Couldn't be wrong about that vest."

"Other men around wearing about the same thing. Huckaby's got a checked shirt on right now—"

"Shirt maybe—but this is a vest. And there's something about the way he stands."

Shawn scrubbed at the sweat clouding his eyes, shifted to ease the muscles of his doubled under legs. "What reason would he have for killing Canfield? Got to have a reason."

Mason shook himself impatiently. "How the hell would I know? Just know he was the one who done it. Maybe he was paid to do it."

"Who'd hate Canfield enough to hire him killed?"

"You called the turn on one—Huckaby."

"He's got reasons, all right—but so have you."

There was a stiffness in Lynch's voice when he replied. "Well, it wasn't me—and that leaves Huckaby. Can't see as it's anything for us to be sweating over anyway. We nab him, turn him over to—"

Lynch's words ended as again a door slammed, this time at the main house. Boot heels rapped sharply on the hardpack. Barney Canfield appeared, coming across the yard,

113

pointing for the man standing beside the black and the hitchrack.

Starbuck crouched lower, pressed forward against the poles of the corral. "Maybe here's where we get some answers," he murmured.

18

Canfield, a fresh cigar clamped between his teeth, passed in front of the unused corral in which Shawn and Mason Lynch huddled, so near he was almost within reach. There was a slackness to the rancher's face, a look of relief, as that of a man coming to the end of a long and tedious journey.

"Ready, eh?" he said, halting beside the man with the black. Turning his head, he threw a glance to the Mexican yard-hand, made a gesture toward the barn. "Vamoose, *hombre*. Go find yourself a job somewheres."

The Mexican shrugged, ambled off in the direction of the barn.

"Ready as I'll ever be," the man in the checked vest said.

"Best thing," Canfield said in a confidential way. "You ain't around—you ain't apt to get in no trouble. Where'll you be—just in case I want you?"

"Across the border—little town called San Plomo. Been there a couple of times before. Plenty of *señoritas* and plenty of that Mex brandy."

"Maybe too much. Stuff can loosen a man's tongue"

"Never got that much yet. Wouldn't make no difference, anyhow. Most of the Mexes there are friends of mine, and what's not don't savvy anything but their own lingo. Don't work up a sweat over it."

"I won't," Barney Canfield said. "Some place special in this San Plomo burg you'll be living?"

"Corrasco's—just ask anybody for him. Sounds like maybe you are figuring on paying me a call, asking things like that."

"Nothing for sure—just never know what might turn up. I—"

The cook came from his kitchen, glanced about, and locating Canfield, started toward him at the painful, halting gait of an old bronc-stomper, crippled by his trade, now compelled to follow a less rigorous way of life.

"Mr. Canfield, when's them fellows coming? Got everything all set."

Conversation between the rancher and the rider had ceased at the cook's appearance. Canfield removed the cigar from his mouth, spat.

"They'll be along, George. You in a hurry?"

"Nope—sure ain't going nowheres. Sort of like to keep my vittles tasty, howsomever."

"They'll eat them, no matter what."

The cook, head cocked to one side, was staring at the departing rider. "You leaving?"

"Sending him out to look over some new range," Canfield replied quickly before the other man could speak. "Aim to be adding to the herd. Got to have more grass."

The cook jutted his chin at the blanket roll cinched tight behind the rider's cantle. "If you'll be gone for a spell, you'll be needing grub."

Checked-vest shrugged. "Figured to swing by on my way out."

George nodded, sucked at his colorless lips. "How long'll you be gone?"

"Couple, maybe three days."

The older man bobbed his head. "It'll be in a sack, laying on the table, if it happens I ain't handy," he said and turning, hobbled off toward his kitchen.

Canfield watched him briefly, until he was out of earshot, then came back to the rider. "Best you forget that. Pick yourself up some supplies next town you hit. Huckaby and the others'll be here in a few minutes."

"I'm ready to pull out soon's I've got my money."

Canfield shifted his cigar to the opposite corner of his mouth, flicked a glance at the kitchen, then to the bunkhouse. No one was in sight, and apparently reassured, he dug inside his shirt front, withdrew a leather pouch. Shielding his movements with his body, he passed the bag to the man in the checked vest.

"Thousand there—gold and bills."

The rider hefted the pouch in his left hand as if calculating its weight. "How much gold? Don't cotton to paper money. Some places just plain won't take it."

"About half. Be no trouble if you work it right. Stop in the first bank you come to on your way south, swap it for gold. Don't be a damned fool and try changing it all in the same place—they might get the idea you'd pulled a hold-up somewhere. Go to three or four different banks."

"Lot of trouble. Would've been better if it was all gold."

"Scraped up what I could. Didn't have much time."

The rider shrugged, tucked the pouch inside his shirt, leisurely rebuttoned it. "You and me are all square now for what I borrowed?"

"Every nickel," Canfield said. "You don't owe me nothing. All them advance wages, all them loans I gave you to pay off your debts are wiped out. We're even."

Shawn Starbuck had listened to the conversation in grim silence, aware that Mason also was equally shocked. It was evident that the man in the checked vest was the one Lynch had seen shoot down Kit Canfield—and it was just as clear that Barney had hired him to do it. One brother murdering another . . . Cain and Abel. To Shawn, spending his life searching for a brother, it was hard to understand how such could come to pass.

Everything that Barney had said and done in town had been pure play-acting, designed to cover over the crime he had planned and brought to be. Whether he had long schemed to rid himself of his brother—stepbrother, in reality—in order to have the Box C all for himself, or had simply taken advantage of Mason Lynch's return to strike, there was no way of knowing. The timely appearance of Lynch—a convicted killer of one Canfield, and a known hater of all—unquestionably fit perfectly into whatever he had in mind.

It had worked out well for him. Kit had been murdered and Mason Lynch had fled. Townspeople, the merchants, his own hired hands, Marshal Virg Huckaby himself had accepted what appeared to be strong evidence—actual proof in the eyes of some—that Mason was the killer, and the posse had taken to the saddle at once determined to run him to earth.

It wouldn't have mattered to Barney Canfield, Shawn realized, whether Mason Lynch was caught and hanged on the spot, or brought in alive to face justice. Mason, with the stain of one Canfield killing already upon his brow, would stand no chance when it was pointed out he still felt his family had been swindled by the three brothers, had declared so publicly. A judge and jury would fall for such simple, straightforward logic and Mason would again pay a stiff price—perhaps with his life this time.

But something had happened that morning to disturb the web Barney Canfield had woven, and set up an uneasiness in the man. It could have been something as simple

117

and ordinary as hunger. Huckaby, perhaps noting that his posse members had been given no opportunity for taking breakfast, and, understandably, in need of food, suggested that time out should be taken to repair that oversight. And as the Box C was the nearest source for food, the men should go there.

Canfield would have had no choice except to agree, but the knowledge that the man he'd hired to kill his brother was still on the premises, and as yet unpaid for his sanguinary labors, dawned upon him. Such opened up any number of dire possibilities—chief among them being a slip of the tongue on the part of the murderer after which the truth would find its way out.

He had then hurried on ahead on the pretext of advising his cook of their coming and seeing to it that all would be in readiness so no undue loss of time would occur. His real purpose had been one of a wholly different nature, however—that of paying off the killer and getting him off the ranch before the posse could arrive.

That, likely, was as close to the true story of what and how it had happened as he could guess, Shawn concluded. And now that he had it squared away in his mind to his conscience's satisfaction, he felt he could make a move, do what must be done. The killer could not be allowed to ride off—that was certain. In some way he must be delayed, held until Virg Huckaby arrived.

"That sonofabitch," he heard Mason Lynch mutter. "Was him all the time—Barney. Had Kit shot down, then unloaded the blame on me. I'm going to—"

"Easy," Shawn cautioned, laying his hand on Mason's arm. "Anything that's done now we want the marshal in on. Only way we can be sure you won't be faulted again."

Lynch drew back. "You mean we ought to just set here, wait for that posse? Hell, that killer'll be long gone by then. It's what Barney came back for—get him out of the way."

"We can't let him get away but the minute we make a move, we'll have all hell on our hands. Canfield gives one yell and all the hired hands on the place come boiling out to help him. Far as they know, you're the killer and it'll look to them like you're here to put a bullet in Barney—with me siding you. They've all got me pegged for a gunslinger hired to help."

Mason relaxed. "Guess you're right, but I ain't seen nobody else around but the cook and that Mex yard hand."

"What about the night crew? Won't they be in the bunkhouse?"

Mason nodded. "Forgot about them. Been so long since I was around a ranch, sort of slipped my mind. Yeh, they'll be there. Probably a half-dozen men—maybe more. Makes the odds plenty bad."

"If we had some way to keep Barney and the killer quiet. Expect we'll need to hold them for only a few minutes. Huckaby and that posse can't be far off." Shawn paused, aware of Mason's probing gaze. "Something bothering you?"

Lynch smiled in a strange, wry manner. "You talking about holding them—maybe having to step out there and pin down eight, even ten guns, just the pair of us—that's what. It'll be one hell of a long shot with the odds all wrong—and you sure don't owe me nothing, not after the way I've done. Best thing you can do is sit tight, not go risking your hide. I made this trouble for myself. Up to me to handle it."

"I'll own up there's lots of places I'd rather be right now than here," Starbuck said wryly. "But a man's bound to help when he has to—and wrong's wrong no matter who it happens to."

"Stay out of town—I want you to be damn sure of that!"

Barney Canfield's voice lifted suddenly as if spurred by anger. Shawn tensed, watched the man in the checked vest reach for the rope linking the black to the hitchrack. He and Mason would have to act; the posse would not be arriving in time.

"Quit fretting about it. I'll be lining out due south. First town I'll hit will be Rock Crossing—then it'll be Tucson. What about old George? Ain't he liable to fuss about me not coming by for that sack of grub?"

"I'll get in there, hide it. He'll think you came in when he wasn't around. *Adios.*"

"*Adios,*" the rider said, and started to mount.

Starbuck touched Mason's arm lightly, drew his pistol and sprang upright.

"Forget it," he said in a hard, low-pitched voice and vaulted over the top bar of the old corral. "You're both standing where you are until the marshal gets here."

19

Barney Canfield's jaw sagged. His eyes flared in surprise. The man with him fell back a step, arm going down smoothly, fingers reaching for the pistol on his hip.

"Don't—" Shawn warned softly.

The rider froze. Starbuck risked a side glance at Lynch. Mason was crouched beside him, weapon steady and leveled. There had been a bad moment when he thought the man, out of pure hate, was going to lose control, start shooting and arouse the others on the ranch; but he had not and now seemed to be all right.

"Keep your hands where I can see them," Starbuck said, adding quickly, "No—not up!" when Canfield started to extend his arms above his head. Anyone looking toward them from the bunkhouse, or elsewhere in the yard, would simply think they were four men in conversation; with arms raised they would immediately realize something else was taking place.

Canfield, fists clenching and releasing at his sides nervously, glared at Shawn. "You must be loco! You think you can hold a gun on me right here in my own yard and get away with it?"

"We're doing it," Mason said laconically.

"Not for long!" the rancher countered. "Right about now I'd say three, maybe four of my boys have got you lined up in their sights. All I've got to do is give them the signal—"

"And you're a dead man—right along with us," Starbuck finished coldly.

Sweat was standing out in large beads on Canfield's forehead. He slid a look at the man in the checked vest, shook his head.

"What's this all about?" he demanded, striving to make

his voice carry a note of indignation. "You here to finish me off—kill off the last of the Canfields?"

Shawn laughed humorlessly. "You're too late with that crock of bull, friend. Mason saw your hired gun there shoot down your brother. We both watched you pay him off and heard you tell him to get out of the country. We're holding the pair of you until Huckaby gets here. So what's it sound like to you?"

"A pack of goddam lies—that's what! Me—have my own brother bushwhacked? You're worse than plain loco!"

"Maybe so, but it tots to something that's pure sense and easy to figure, and I reckon it will to the marshal and his posse when they get here, too."

The rider with Canfield shifted gently on his feet. "Well, I ain't in the notion to hang around and find out," he drawled. "And the way things are, I guess I'll just climb onto my horse and ride on."

Starbuck's jaw hardened. "Be a mistake to try."

"Misdoubt that. There's two of us and two of you. I figure that jailbird ain't much good with a gun, him not having much to do with one for a long time. On top of that I can see a couple of the boys a-watching us. Way I see it, odds are all in my favor."

"And far as Huckaby's concerned," Barney Canfield put in, "it's going to be maybe another half-hour before he shows up—and you sure ain't going to be able to hold us here like this for that long."

"You think we can't?" Shawn asked quietly. "Make your move—find out."

But he knew Canfield was right. Standing in the open, in full view of anyone on the ranch, they were in a desperate situation. It was only necessary for some of the Box C men to grow suspicious, circle the buildings, and come in on them from the rear. He and Mason were then as good as dead.

Shawn centered his attention on the rider with Canfield. If trouble came now it would come from him; he had the look of wildness in his eyes, the offhanded way of a man not afraid to dare the risks.

"Got to move them out of here," he said to Mason. "Need to get under cover—fast."

"We could back them into the barn, hold them in one of the stalls."

"How about that hostler? He in there?"

"I see him working in one of the corrals, out back."

Starbuck bobbed his head at the rancher and his hired

121

gun. "Start walking," he ordered, motioning with his weapon.

The two came away from the rack slowly. Sweat was glistening on their faces, and they carried themselves loosely, arms hung forward. Immediately Starbuck stepped to the side, endeavoring to block the view of anyone looking from the upper yard.

"Get there at the door," Shawn said to Mason. "I'll herd them by—you take their guns—"

Lynch nodded his understanding, started to cross over, going in between the two men and the horse standing at the rack.

"Watch out!" Starbuck warned suddenly, seeing the danger.

In that same instant the man in the checked vest lunged backwards, smashed hard into Mason. Spinning, he drew his pistol, made a dive for the shelter of the small shed a long stride away.

Shawn fired as he saw the rider whip up his gun, lay a shot at him. He couldn't see Barney Canfield, knew only that the rancher had flung himself to the opposite direction, where Lynch, caught against the black gelding, was struggling to regain his balance.

Guns blasted from behind him. He heard a groan but there was no time to wheel, see if it was Mason or Canfield who'd been hit. The man behind the shed was firing at him now and someone near the bunkhouse was opening up. The shots had brought the rest of the Box C crew into the fight.

Ducking low, he lunged for protection of the log water trough a short distance to his right. Bullets dug into the hard-packed soil around his feet, whirred by him, thudded dully into the wall of the barn beyond him. He heard someone yelling and then the rider behind the shed stepped fully into the open. His pistol was leveled. The big, round O of the weapon's muzzle seemed only an arm's length away.

Shawn dipped low, threw himself forward, fired as he went down. The man buckled, clutched at his chest. He staggered back, fell behind the shed.

Shawn rolled frantically, gained the protection of the trough. His pistol was empty, he was sure. Heaving for breath, he lay full length, began to rod the spent casings from the forty-five's cylinder, glanced to his left. Mason, prone in the dust, one arm bloodied and tight against his side, was endeavoring to crawl to the barn. Bullets were stabbing into the ground about him.

Shawn, his weapon reloaded, came to a crouch, and keeping low, broke clear of the water trough and ran toward Lynch. He reached the man's side, bent swiftly, caught him under the arms. Ignoring the crackling guns, he started for the barn, eyes only absently noticing Barney Canfield's crumpled shape near the hitchrack.

Shocking pain in his leg, hot and numbing, brought him to a halt. Taking a firmer grasp of Mason, he tried to continue, discovered his leg would not respond.

"Get away from me!"

He became aware of Mason's voice, yelling at him through the dust and drifting smoke.

"Leave me be—ain't a chance of me making it!"

Shawn shook his head stubbornly, released his grip on the man's arms. If he stayed low, he'd not be so easy a target. Flat on his belly, he extended his hand to Lynch.

"Hang on—I'll drag you—"

"No—dammit—you go on—"

Starbuck seized Lynch by the wrist, began to work his way toward the open doorway of the now close-by structure. Another bullet ripped into him, catching him high in the shoulder, paralyzing his muscles, causing him to drop his weapon. Releasing his hold on Mason, he twisted around, tried to recover the forty-five—recoiled as a booted foot stamped down upon it.

Grim, he looked up. Barney Canfield, pistol clutched so tightly in his hand the knuckles showed white, blood streaking his face where a bullet had stunned him—but only temporarily—was standing over him.

"Damn the both of you!" he yelled in a trembling voice. "You ain't telling nobody—nothing!"

Starbuck jerked back, attempted to get his hand upon the weapon trapped beneath the rancher's foot—winced as the deafening report of a pistol slammed against his eardrums. But there was no shocking impact of a bullet, no pain. He brushed at the sweat and dust blinding him. Canfield had twisted half about, was staring with unseeing eyes at Mason Lynch. Smoke trickled from the barrel of the weapon in his hand. His glance caught Shawn's and he smiled grimly as Canfield stumbled off to one side, fell heavily.

"Wasn't as dead—as he figured," he mumbled.

Starbuck lay back, probed the dust for his pistol, found it. Men were running toward them . . . several men. Shawn pulled himself to a sitting position, wondering at the absence of gunshots. The Box C crew wouldn't let it end there. Ignoring the woodenness of his arm, the dull

123

burning in his leg, he squared himself around, prepared to make a fight of it.

The first man he saw was Huckaby. Behind him came Kemmer, and the one they'd called Ike. On beyond them others of the posse were mingling with Canfield's men. The old cook, hands wrapped in his apron, was standing nearby watching it all in a dazed sort of way.

Starbuck, throwing everything he had into it, worked himself to his knees, managed then to get on his feet. He saw a look of concern cross Mason's face.

"It's all right. It's done with," he said. "The posse's here."

"Thank God," Lynch murmured, letting himself go limp.

"Drop that gun, Starbuck!"

At the sound of Huckaby's harsh command, a bleakness settled over Shawn. He allowed his weapon to fall, watched as the lawman turned, looked to the upper end of the yard.

"Hayman—over here! Want these two patched up. They've got some answering to do."

Huckaby moved in, scooped up Mason's pistol and then Starbuck's, held them in one hand by the barrels. Near by Fred Kemmer was bending over the man lying behind the shed, while beyond Ike and another member of the posse were crouched beside Barney Canfield.

"Finished it, I see," the marshal said in a dry, angry way to Mason Lynch. "You killed him—the last one of them—just like you aimed to."

Starbuck stirred impatiently as an understanding of the lawman's attitude and words filtered into his wearied and numbed brain.

"Can see there never was any doubt in your mind," he said. "You had it pegged as Mason all the time."

"Not hard figuring it out."

"And you're a man who's never wrong—"

"That mean something?"

"Only that you think you're so damned right that you'll nail Mason and me to the cross without even trying to find out what happened."

"I got eyes—I can see," Huckaby said stubbornly.

"The hell with what you can see, you'd best be hunting for the truth! Looks don't mean a thing, most of the time. You want to know something—I figured you for the killer because it seemed to me you had the best reason."

Huckaby straightened in outrage. "Me! Why would I—"

"Anybody could see Kit Canfield was riding you raw. Hate you had in your eyes yesterday said you'd as soon kill him as draw a breath."

"Well, it wasn't me—and you can mark that down in red chalk! And if this is all because you're trying to cover over for your friend there, start something—forget it. I've got you both cold-turkey."

"You've got nothing, Marshal, far as we're concerned. Man laying over there behind that shed is the one who killed Kit. Barney hired him. Mason was there, saw it happen."

The lawman frowned, clawed at his chin as he turned to Lynch, now sitting up and being attended to by the man called Hayman. "You seen it?"

Mason moved his head slowly, weakly. The loss of blood was telling on him. "At the Frisco House. Fellow walked up to Kit, shot him. Then got away."

Huckaby glanced at the men drifting in from the opposite end of the yard. "Damned funny you didn't come tell me about it," he said in a suspicious voice. "Why didn't you?"

Mason managed a tired smile. "You know the answer to that—I'd never have got the chance to talk. Some of your good citizens would've strung me up before I got my mouth open."

Fred Kemmer moved in to stand beside Huckaby. "Still no proof you're telling the truth. Everybody's dead that was mixed up in it except you two—and a dead man sure can't tell his side of the story."

"It's the truth, just the same," Starbuck said angrily. Hayman, who seemed to have some rudimentary skills in medicine, or possibly was a veterinarian, was working on his arm now. "If it wasn't he'd never come back with me. He was headed for Mexico. I caught up, talked him into forgetting that, trying instead to clear his name."

"A good yarn," Huckaby said, indifferently. "Makes more sense, however, to think you both came here for one thing—kill Barney, finish what you started."

"Barney ain't dead yet, Marshal," one of the men hunched over the rancher called, looking up. "He can talk, maybe."

"Make him," Starbuck said bluntly, and then recalled something that had slipped his mind—something that should help convince Huckaby and the others of the truth. "Money he paid off with is inside the dead man's shirt. Leather pouch. There'll be a thousand dollars in it—gold and paper. We heard them talking about it."

Huckaby, flashing a look at Shawn, wheeled away, crossed to where Barney Canfield lay sprawled face up. Starbuck watched the lawman kneel, slip a hand under the rancher's head, raise it slightly. Kemmer had returned to the shed, was rummaging about on the rider's body for the pouch. He found it.

"Reckon he's got hisself an answer," Mason said as Huckaby lowered Canfield's head to the ground, stood up. "Be like that bastard to say it was me, no matter if he was dying," he added bitterly.

The lawman remained motionless, staring down at the rancher for several moments, and then slowly he turned, came back to where Starbuck and Mason Lynch waited.

"Guess you were telling the truth," he said in a begrudging voice as he handed them back their pistols. "Barney wanted Kit out of the way so's the ranch would be his. Hired the killing done. All there was to it."

A surge of resentment shook Shawn Starbuck. *All there was to it!* That was a hell of a thing for a lawman to say! The affair had almost cost Mason and him their lives— and it would have meant a lynching for Mason if the posse had been able to catch him during those past few hours. Perhaps for him, too, if Canfield had been able to convince the men that he was Lynch's hired gun.

But it was over now. Mason could go his way—either on to the Mescals or remain and see if he did have some claim on the Box C; and likely he could square things with the girl, Marie, go ahead with plans interrupted over ten years ago.

As for himself he could continue with his reason for being in the Rockinstraw Valley country. He turned to Kemmer, standing nervously by, looking down in that self-conscious way of a man caught in a bad mistake, pointed to the group of Canfield riders loitering in the yard.

"Which one is Jim Ivory?"

Kemmer's brows drew together. He shook his head. "Ivory? He ain't one of them—he's the one laying dead there behind the shed."

20

Starbuck stood absolutely motionless, transfixed. Somewhere deep inside him his breath had locked and he felt as if he had been struck a powerful blow to the midsection. The man in the checked vest—the killer—he was Jim Ivory. His own brother, perhaps. . . .

Vaguely he heard Huckaby's voice calling to several of the men to hitch up a surrey, a team and wagon. The words jarred him, stirred him from the paralytic lethargy that gripped him. He turned, moved slowly to the shed, halted. Jim Ivory lay on his back, face bared to the streaming sunlight, eyes half closed. His hat had come off, revealing a thick shock of dark hair. Lying under him, partly visible, was a scattered pack of worn cards, apparently having spilled from his pocket when he fell. A deuce of hearts . . . nine of clubs . . . an ace . . .

A man always with a deck of cards on him.

Shawn recalled again what he had been told about Jim Ivory. Continually ready for a game . . . would play himself if no one else was willing or handy. Gambling had been his curse, it would seem; the debts Barney Canfield had mentioned had likely come from his losses. But the man was Jim Ivory, and Ivory—possibly—was Ben Starbuck, and if true, he had shot down his own brother.

Abruptly Shawn's jaw came to a hard line. The cool, practical streak that ordinarily governed him shook off all the speculating, all the conjecture, the weighing of probabilities. Ignoring the throbbing pain in his arm, favoring his stiffening leg, he stepped up to the lifeless body, knelt beside it, looked more closely at the flaccid features.

The hooded eyes were blue. The hair was dark, and there was a blockiness to the face. Taut, Starbuck reached out, placed his fingers on the left brow, pushed aside the thick growth.

There was no scar. No scar where Ben had one.

Relief shot through him. He hesitated a long moment, looked again, knowing that he must be absolutely certain or forever have his doubts. There was no telltale, identifying mark. Slowly he pulled back, painfully got to his feet, sweat clothing him in a solid sheet as a mountainous worry slid from his shoulders. He wheeled then to face the curious stares of the men gathered around.

"Is it him?" Mason Lynch's voice was anxious.

Shawn moved his head. "No—it's not him."

He saw Mason's shoulders go down in a relieved, exhausted sort of way, heard him murmur once more: "Thank God . . ."

Starbuck echoed the words silently. For the first time in his life he was glad the man he had hoped would be his brother—was not. A spring wagon rattled up from the rear of the barn, halted beside Barney Canfield's body. As several men, directed by Huckaby, bent to lift the rancher into the bed, a second vehicle, a black surrey, came from the same direction, stopped near Mason.

Two members of the posse stepped up to Lynch, helped him aboard. Another beckoned to Shawn. Suddenly very tired, he moved toward the two-seater, idly listening to Lynch give instructions as to where their horses could be found, and directing they be taken to Pete Fortney's livery stable for care. The voices responding to Mason were friendly, sounded pleased to be of help. Mason Lynch was home again, Starbuck realized; he had been taken back into the fold.

As for himself—he stared off into the hot blue of the empty sky to the east. Las Cruces lay in that general direction. He'd have to take it easy for a few days, allow his wounds to heal, then he'd head out. Maybe next time—next time he'd find Ben.